Once Upon a Midnight Dreary

An Enchanted Realms Novel

MICHELLE MILES

TOLHEIM
SEA
Port
Leclare
Crou
Holl
Rothshi
ROTH
CASSONÉ
Elder
Driftbell
Thornhurst
Castle

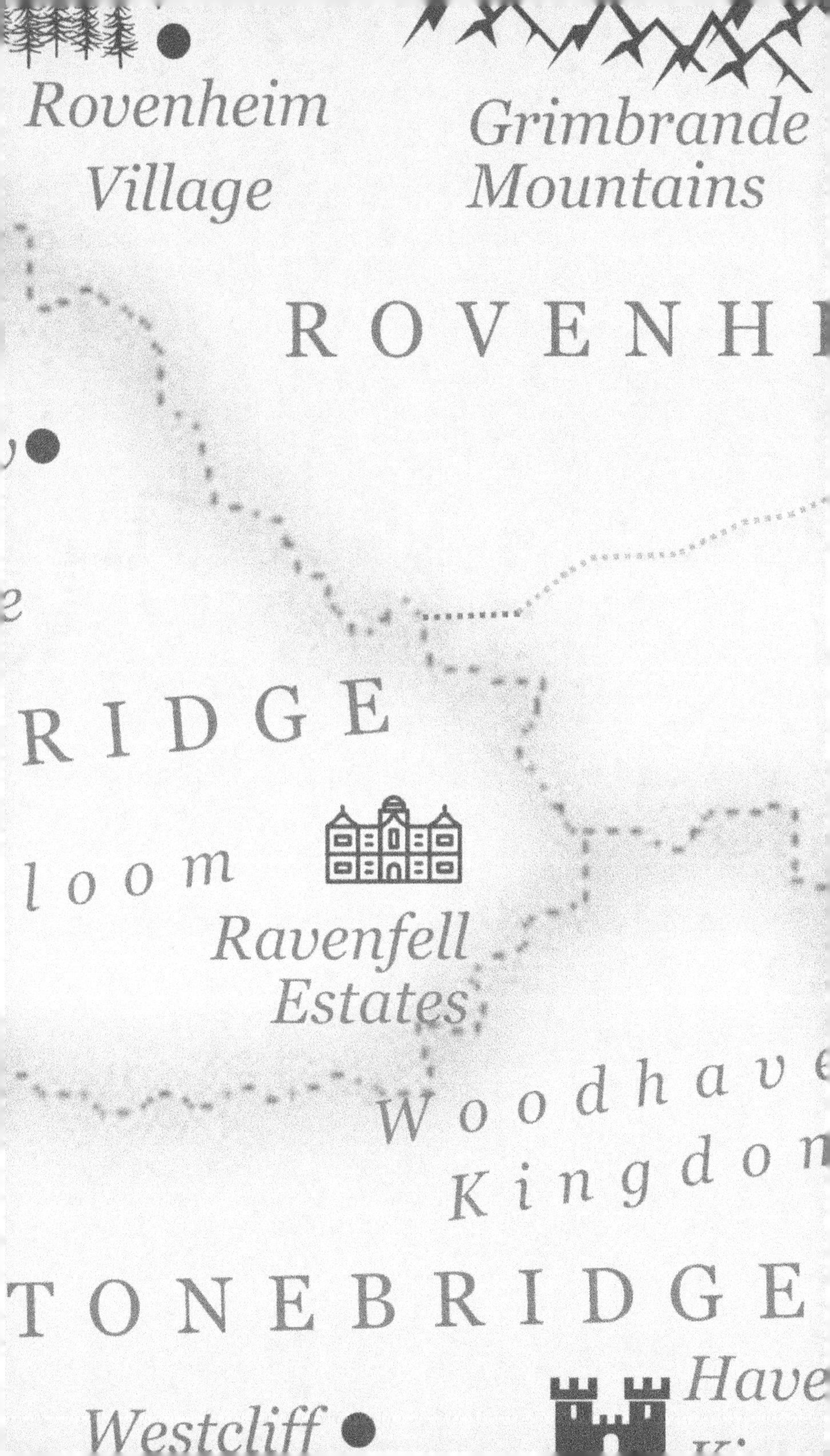

Rovenheim
Village
Grimbrande
Mountains
ROVENHE
RIDGE
loom
Ravenfell
Estates
Woodhave
Kingdom
TONEBRIDGE
Westcliff
Have

For anyone who's ever stared at a raven and thought, "Yes, but what if it's a love story?"

PROLOGUE

Late October, Present Day

Willowmere Restorative Retreat nestled in the hills outside Drumchapel Village was like a hidden oasis among the trees. The autumn wind rustled the branches, loosening crisp leaves that fluttered to the ground and cluttered the sidewalk. Marigold's booted feet shuffled through them—*swish, swish*—as she made her way toward the concrete steps, passing the small, hand-painted sign that read *Keep Off the Grass*.

She paused, gazing up at the stone façade draped in climbing ivy. It looked more like a forgotten estate house than a private wellness retreat. Aunt Hilde had checked herself in several days ago—something Marigold only learned by accident. Her mother had failed to mention it, but Marigold had overheard the hushed phone call when she was supposed to be upstairs finishing her homework.

She'd skipped her afternoon classes, caught the bus from the village, and walked the long country road to reach the foot of the hills. Willowmere didn't exactly welcome outsiders, but that wasn't going to stop her. She was set to see her favorite aunt.

The wind lifted her long blonde hair, making it flutter in her face. She tucked a wayward lock behind her ear as she trudged up the stairs and entered, pulling open the tinted glass door and stepping inside.

A woman sat behind an oversized, half-oval shaped wood desk. She glanced up when Marigold entered, her curious gaze landing on her. She spoke into a headset while her fingers tapped away on the keyboard. The sign on the desk read *Reception*.

Suddenly, Marigold wanted to flee. But determination pushed her onward to see her aunt. Taking a deep breath, she stepped up to the desk. The woman finished her phone call and then greeted her with a smile, her dark red lips pulling up at the corners.

"How can I help you, miss?"

"I'm here to see my aunt, Hilde."

Dark brows winged upward. "Do you have an appointment?"

Her courage started to wane. "No."

"One moment." She pulled off her headset and stood. "Wait here."

The woman in a pale blue dress bustled around a corner, disappearing. Marigold chewed her lower lip as she glanced around the spacious waiting room. The walls were a warm green color, mimicking the outdoors. The furnishings were well-worn but comfortable. An oversized velvet chair in a rich honey color sat opposite a two-seat sofa in a similar color. Magazines scattered across the glass coffee table. In one corner, a water cooler with cone-shaped cups.

She was about to take a seat when the woman returned.

"I spoke with the director," she announced. "She'll be along in a moment to speak with you."

Marigold's palms broke into a hot sweat. What if they didn't allow her to see her aunt? What if they turned her away? What then? She gave a sideways glance at the door, thinking about the long trek back home and having to tell her mother she had skipped school for no good reason. Long, quiet minutes ticked by.

"Miss?"

Marigold turned to greet the tall woman heading her way. She was slender, with a fall of pale silver hair over one shoulder. The strands were thick and luxurious. Her chin came to a point, and her cheekbones were high and angled, giving her a face that looked as though it was carved from marble.

She smiled as she extended a hand. "I'm Director Aveen. What's your name?"

"Marigold. I came to see my aunt. She checked in a few days ago."

"Yes, I'm familiar with Hilde. We have a strict no-visitors policy." She paused there, pressing her lips together in a thin straight line.

"But your aunt...well, when she heard you were here, she insisted I bring you to her."

"She did?"

She nodded and motioned toward a hallway. "If you'll follow me."

Marigold fell in step behind Director Aveen down the long hallway. At the end, she turned left and led her to a door. There, she pushed it open and stepped aside to allow her to exit.

"You'll find her in the courtyard." She granted her a smile before she stepped back and let the door swing closed behind her.

Marigold stood there, her eyes scanning the area. The enclosed courtyard was a cool, shaded place that unfolded like a secret garden. Sunlight filtered through the autumn trees, dappling the mossy flagstone pathway that wound around. Ivy climbed the crumbling walls, rising up to conceal the cracked mortar.

In the center, a fountain bubbled happily, topped by a fairy reaching for the sky, her stone wings spread behind her. Strange flowers grew in stone pots along the walls, their petals open and reaching for the dapple of sunlight. Wind chimes made of crystal tinkled in the faint breeze, their melody soft and enchanting.

Marigold followed the winding path around the fountain, and there, at the far end, was her aunt. She sat in a cushioned iron chair in a puddle of light. Behind her, a large tree with its silvery leaves hanging over her as though a silent sentry. A shawl crocheted with shimmery threads was wrapped around her shoulders. For a moment, she looked like part of the garden, as though rooted here in the place where time forgot.

She lifted her gaze to her as Marigold approached, a weak smile on her lips. For the first time, she noticed how aged her aunt looked. Deep lines creased down her cheeks and crinkled at the corners of her eyes. Fatigue was there, too, as though she hadn't slept in ages. And there was something strange about the way the light in her eyes seemed dimmer. Less alive. Less vibrant.

She held out a hand to her. "There she is, my lovely girl."

Marigold grasped her hand in hers and noticed how fragile she felt.

"When the director told me you were here, I thought it was a cruel joke," she said with a half laugh. She released her hand and motioned to a similar chair opposite her. "Have a seat."

"The director said you insisted on seeing me."

She nodded. "I did. But aren't you supposed to be in school?"

Marigold glanced down at her hands folded in her lap to keep the truth from showing on her face. She had no intention of telling her aunt she'd skipped classes to come.

"Ah, so you are. What will your mother say?"

Her head snapped up as her heart rammed hard in her chest. "You aren't going to tell her, are you?"

"No, dearest. It will be our secret. What are you doing here?"

"I had to see how you were. I overheard Mom talking to you on the phone."

"I see. She didn't tell you I was here?"

"No." Marigold twisted her hands together in her lap. She glanced around the courtyard. "What *is* this place, auntie? It smells...old. It looks ancient. Like something out of a storybook."

She chuckled. "It's an old sanctuary for people like me who have been away from home too long. Don't you worry. I'll be good as new soon enough."

Marigold drew her brows together in question. "What do you mean, away from home? Isn't your home near ours?"

A smile tugged at the corners of her mouth. "Home is where memories are created and stories are told."

Marigold relaxed, leaning back on the thick cushion of the chair. "Are you going to tell me a story, then?"

"If you have time and are in the mood," she said with a grin.

Excitement edged through her. "I'm always in the mood for one of your stories, auntie. What's this one about?"

Thoughtfulness creased her features as she decided what to tell her. "How about one about a haunted estate, where nothing is as it seems? A woman who inherits that estate and a brooding man who guards the manor with a secret as heavy as stone."

"That sounds intriguing," Marigold said.

"There's also a raven that whispers and watches, its wings tied to a centuries-old curse."

"*Another* story about a curse?"

"Oh, yes. There are *many* stories about curses."

A shiver raced up her spine. Marigold tugged her coat closer. "That seems fitting for this time of year."

"Very well, then. Once upon a time, there was a beautiful heiress named Victoria who moved into a crumbling manor..."

CHAPTER 1

The letter arrived on black-edged stationery at half-past nine during breakfast on a too-bright day for mourning.

Victoria Ravenwood stared down at the unfamiliar wax seal stamped with the sigil of a bird in flight. A raven, from the looks of it. A slanting, looping hand had scrawled her name across the front in black ink.

Miss Victoria Ravenwood
Care of Mr. Hubert Pembroke, Crown Hollow, Rothbridge

"What is it, dear?" Aunt Eloise peered over her teacup, her bright blue eyes alight with interest. She looked like a feral cat ready to pounce on the latest juicy gossip.

"A letter."

She laughed. "Of course, it's a letter, silly goose. What does it say?"

She was always a bit of a busybody. Victoria didn't want to read the contents of the letter in front of her. She'd demand to know it word for word. As her thumb swept over the seal, she had the distinct feeling this was meant for her and her alone.

Why she felt that way, she did not know.

It had no return address, which she found curious.

"Well? What is it, dear?"

She granted her aunt a faint smile as she placed her napkin next to her half-empty plate and pushed back from the table. "I think I'll read it in the parlor."

Alone. She wanted to read it alone, and not with her aunt breathing down her neck.

The woman harrumphed as she hastened from the dining room. No doubt she was planning to extort the information from her later.

Aunt Eloise meant well, but she was overbearing and pushy. Victoria was grateful to her and her uncle for taking her in after her parents died, but the woman was exhausting on a good day. If there was news of any sort in the contents of the letter, she would never let it rest.

What news, though? Victoria, still in mourning, walked to the parlor and pulled the door closed. She stood in the silence of the room staring down at that raven wax seal wondering about the sender. As far as she knew, there was no one else who knew she was here. She had no family except for her aunt, who was her mother's older sister, and her uncle by marriage. And she didn't exactly have a lot of friends.

Moving to the sofa, she popped the seal. Perching on the edge, she unfolded the letter with a careful hand. She pulled in a deep breath when she read it and then read it again.

This couldn't be right.

Could it?

To Miss Ravenwood,

In accordance with the last will and testament of your late parents, Abner and Eleanor Ravenwood, you are hereby named sole heir to their estate, which includes Ravenfell Manor in the village of Elderbloom, Rothbridge. You are requested to take possession immediately.

There were other instructions about inheritance, land deeds, and legal oversight. It was signed by an *R. Williams, Solicitor, Brown, Williams & Davis.* She had never heard of him.

Her mind drifted away from the letter and the solicitor. To her childhood home and a place she thought she'd never see again. She thought her parents had sold it when she was a child.

Ravenfell Manor.

Her nightmares of the manor had long since faded, but now, as she held the letter, they flooded back to her.

A piano that played a haunting tune when no one was about. The acrid scent of smoke drifting through the halls. A shift in temperature from warm and comfortable to cold and frightening.

Sometimes during certain times of the year, a misty fog curled through the west wing corridor.

What she recalled most of all was the man in the shadows with eyes full of sorrow and despair.

Her parents had never seen him.

But she had. And she had never feared him.

When she was eight years old, they fled Ravenfell Manor under the cover of darkness. And now, twenty years later, it had returned to her.

Perhaps her fortune had changed. As the heiress of the country estate, she had a home to call her own. She no longer needed to depend upon the kindness of her aging aunt and uncle.

It was a moment of elation.

Shattered by the opening of the parlor door.

Her aunt bustled in with an expectant look on her face. Victoria wasn't so sure she wanted to share the contents of the letter with her, but then, she also knew her aunt would badger her until she did.

"Good news, dear?" she asked, her tone hopeful.

Was it good news? She said nothing as she extended the letter. Aunt Eloise took it and read it, her face an explosion of expressions. From surprise to doubt to sorrow to something akin to envy.

"Well, this *is* a surprise. I thought my sister and her husband sold off that crumbling old manor years ago." She handed back the letter.

"I suppose they didn't."

"Naturally, you'll refuse to move there." She said it flippantly, as if this were already true.

"Why would I do that?" Victoria rose, her ire suddenly raised.

"Well, my dear, you are a single lady. Alone. You can't possibly think of running that estate all by yourself." She chuckled, as though the thought was merely a jest.

She lifted a brow. "Why shouldn't I?"

Aunt Eloise wrung her hands, looking confused. "You are a single lady," she said again.

"Yes, I am. With an inheritance at my disposal. I'm sure I can hire anyone I need to help me run and take care of the estate."

Flabbergasted, she said, "You're considering it?"

Annoyance hit her hard and fast at her aunt's disbelief. She understood very well that she was a young, single lady. With no prospects looming and no purpose to keep her here in Crown Hollow, Victoria saw no reason not to consider it.

"Yes," she said, the word an icy breath.

Her aunt didn't understand her need to find independence. Now, she had a chance—a real chance—at a life all her own. If she stayed in the city with Aunt Eloise, she'd suffocate.

Aunt Eloise remained still as a statue, rooted in the middle of the room, her chest heaving with labored breaths.

"I simply can't allow it," she said then, her tone stern. As though she would entertain no other thoughts on the matter.

Victoria stiffened. "The letter says I'm to take possession imme-diately."

"Who's to say this letter is valid?" Eloise snapped. "Why, I've never heard of this solicitor, and as far as I know, Abner and Eleanor made no mention of this in their wills."

This was not going well. Victoria resisted the urge to crumple the letter in her fist.

"What's all this?" Uncle Hubert's voice trickled in from the doorway.

He stepped around Aunt Eloise, holding his hat and gazing at her with curiosity and question in his eyes. He must have been on his way out the door to his job when he heard the voices in the parlor. Victoria blew out a breath of relief while Aunt Eloise spun to face him, her cheeks red from her indignation.

"It seems our little Victoria is an heiress," she said with a snort, as though it were nothing more than a fiction.

Anger pounded through her veins. How dare she.

Uncle Hubert's gaze flickered to her, one brow raised. In all the years they'd been married, Hubert was the silent, tolerant type. He never argued with his wife. He mostly ignored her. And some-times when he was exasperated, he'd mutter annoyances under his breath.

But he had never been unkind to Victoria. When her parents died unexpectedly and she had nowhere else to go, it was Hubert who offered his home to her. Victoria often wondered if he had to persuade his wife to allow her to move here, or if he had merely expected her acquiescence in his quiet, authoritative way.

He was tall, thin, wiry. With a head full of salt and pepper hair belying his actual age. Kindness and compassion filled his brown eyes as he brushed by his wife and entered the room. He perched on the chair next to her, an encouraging smile on his lips.

"You received this news?" he asked.

"Just today." She handed him the letter.

He read it over, his face impassive. His eyes slipped down the page, then returned to the top and read it again. When he finished his second read-through, he handed it back to her.

"Well, then, I'll make an appointment with Mr. Williams straightaway. We'll go see him together. Today, if possible." He winked as he got to his feet.

Aunt Eloise nearly vibrated out of her skin. "What? Hubert, you can't take this seriously? And what do you mean today? Don't you have work?"

He halted next to her, drawing himself up to his full height, which towered over his curvy wife. "Indeed, I do. And the bank will allow me one afternoon off for an appointment, I should think. I will accompany our niece myself." He cut a glance toward her. "I'll send a note right away. Perhaps he can see us this afternoon. If he can, I'll send the carriage for you."

"Thank you, uncle."

Elation pounded through her. She never expected him to be her strongest ally.

He headed toward the door. Aunt Eloise bustled after him, her skirts swishing with her indignation.

"Hubert, this is preposterous. How can you encourage this? She's a young, single woman. How do you expect her to find a husband on a country estate?"

"I will say no more, wife. And neither will you." He wagged a warning finger at her.

Their voices faded as he walked away, likely heading to his study to write the necessary letter. Victoria imagined the horrified expression on her aunt's face at his stern order. It made her smile.

She folded the letter and rose. If she were going to meet with the solicitor that afternoon, she needed to prepare herself.

True to his word, Uncle Hubert made arrangements for them to meet Mr. Williams at four o'clock in the afternoon. Aunt Eloise was flabbergasted at the late hour of the day, complaining he would miss tea. Hubert seemed unconcerned.

He waited for her at the door, where he offered Victoria his arm. Then they stepped out into the afternoon air.

Her aunt and uncle resided in an elegant red-brick brownstone nestled along one of Crown Hollow's most fashionable avenues—a tree-lined promenade where gas lamps flickered to life each evening and ladies in silk gloves exchanged glances behind parasols. The home, with its wrought-iron railings and polished brass doorknobs, was a testament to his esteemed reputation, if not their sentiment. Her uncle, a man of wealth and measured charm, was a senior partner at one of the oldest banking houses. He attended every society function worth mentioning and knew the names and scandals of everyone who mattered.

Outside the gate, a sleek one-horse carriage waited beside the curb, its dark lacquered body catching the glow of the late afternoon sun. The driver stood stiffly by, gloved hands clasped, while the scent of coal smoke and lilacs drifted through the city air.

"Carson, we're heading to Brown, Williams & Davis on Park Place," Hubert said.

"Very good, sir." Carson opened the door for her as he nodded to her uncle.

As she stepped toward the open carriage door, a sharp caw sounded. A raven fluttered overhead, its wings slicing the sky like a blade before it vanished beyond the rooftops.

Victoria paused.

Normally, she would not notice such things. A bird was just a bird. But today, with a letter in her pocket and the past pressing at her heels, it felt significant.

Once inside, they headed through the busy streets. Victoria clasped her hands in her lap, trying to hide the trembling. She was nervous, her mind filled with questions. What if this was a dream? What if there was some mistake? What if she was truly not inheriting Ravenfell Manor?

"No need to be nervous," Hubert said, as though sensing she was on edge. "I know Mr. Williams."

Her brows rose. "You do?"

"Yes, he was in the bank a few days ago looking to take out a loan to build a second home. Naturally, I agreed." His smile was genuine before he turned serious. "Is this inheritance unexpected?"

His question was not one of prying, but more of concern. Victoria nodded. "I thought my parents sold the Ravenfell estate years ago. I can't imagine why they kept it."

The clop-clop of the horse's hooves came to a slow as the carriage stopped. The driver opened the door. Victoria stepped out onto the sidewalk, the afternoon sun beaming down around her. She lifted her gaze to the stone building where the offices of Brown, Williams & Davis resided. It was tucked between a perfumery and a clockmaker on one of the avenues. The lamplighters were already out, moving down the street like a shadow.

Her uncle was at her side a moment later, taking her by the elbow and leading her into the building with a gentle nudge.

Moments later, they were ushered into Mr. Williams's small but tidy office where they sat in velvet-backed chairs in front of a perfectly organized desk. Mr. Roger Williams was a tall, thin man with wire-rimmed glasses perching on a narrow nose. After a few pleasantries with her uncle, he sat before the polished mahogany desk in the oversized leather chair and folded his hands on top of it.

"I daresay that letter came as a bit of a shock to you, didn't it?" he asked.

"Yes," Victoria replied. She kept her hands clenched together to keep him from seeing her tremble.

"Your father, Abner, was determined to keep his final wishes as quiet as possible."

"Why?" she asked.

"Apparently, Ravenfell Manor has been in your family for generations. He didn't want a distant relative to come sniffing around claiming the title, I gathered, though he never outright said it. Your parents chose to leave the manor several years ago, but the property remains in excellent legal standing." He reached down and opened a drawer, then pulled out a thick folio and laid it on the desk. He pushed it toward her. "The title passes to you now."

She stared at the thick folio as though it were a venomous snake.

"After the death of your grandfather, Henry Ravenwood, the estate was locked in probate for years. Your father had a dickens of a time getting it out of probate. When he realized his father—your grandfather—had written into his estate that only a male heir could take possession, well...your father made sure it would pass to you."

Victoria's mouth went dry. She was their only child. She had no other siblings. And if her father hadn't arranged his last will and testament the way he had, then the estate would have surely gone to a distant cousin.

Knowing her father, there was no way he'd allow that to happen.

"I see," she said at last, still eyeing the thick folder.

"You are to take full possession of the estate in person, Miss Ravenwood," Mr. Williams added.

"And what happens if she doesn't?" Uncle Hubert asked.

Perhaps he sensed her unease. Indeed, her determination had waned a bit after hearing this news. But only a bit.

Mr. Williams's expression did not change. "Then Ravenfell remains sealed. The manor is not to be sold, divided, or otherwise disposed of. It is to remain within the Ravenwood bloodline or fall into ruin." His gaze drifted back to her. "I daresay that would be your father's last wish. To see it fall into ruin."

With a shaking hand, she reached for the folio and flipped it open. A survey of the property was on top, detailing the boundary. A single iron key rested on top of the survey, its teeth long and jagged. Ancient.

Mr. Williams cleared his throat and adjusted his glasses. "There is...one additional matter, Miss Ravenwood. The estate's financial accounts."

She lifted her gaze and met his. "The accounts?"

Next to her, Uncle Hubert shifted in his seat. "Wouldn't those accounts be frozen after all these years?"

Ah, yes, the banker at heart. Of course, he'd ask that question.

Mr. Williams's mouth twitched in a half grin. "One would think. However, your father and grandfather were, shall we say, men who planned for unforeseen events."

He slid a second envelope across the desk to her. This one was thick and sealed with gold wax. The stamp on the seal was that of the Ravenwood sigil—a crowned raven, wings spread outward, perched upon a branch.

"There is a trust in your name. Quietly maintained by the Elderbloom branch of the Royal Bank of Rothbridge."

Uncle Hubert sucked in a quiet breath as she snapped her head in his direction. Her uncle, as it were, worked for the Crown Hollow Royal Bank of Rothbridge.

Williams continued, as though neither of them had reacted. "Interest from assets has accumulated over the last several decades."

"It...has?" she asked, her voice faint. She felt lightheaded all of a sudden. Pinpricks dotted her vision.

The solicitor nodded. "You'll find it more than sufficient to restore Ravenfell to habitability. And perhaps to maintain a small staff, should you require one. Though there is already a caretaker on site. He should be able to assist you with any of your needs."

He said it lightly, as though it were of no consequence someone was already there.

"A caretaker, you say?" Her uncle leaned forward, his elbow on his knee. "Someone lives there already?"

"Yes, of course," Mr. Williams replied.

Victoria was aware of the wary glance her uncle gave her. She was also aware that moving into a crumbling estate with a mysterious caretaker was probably not the best idea.

But she would see it through, no matter what.

"Shall I set up an appointment for you at the bank?" he asked.

Her uncle started to answer, but she jumped in. "Yes, please. That would be helpful."

"Do you have any other questions?" the solicitor asked.

She granted him a smile. "No, Mr. Williams. You've been generous with your time. Thank you for everything."

She picked up the thick envelope with the banking information along with the folio and rose. Her uncle got to his feet. She sensed unease coming from him. They bid the solicitor farewell and headed back into the late afternoon.

Chapter 2

Two days later, Victoria packed her meager belongings. Her aunt was beside herself. She was determined to keep Victoria from leaving and heading to Elderbloom with her inheritance. It took her uncle, as the voice of reason, to talk her down from her near hysteria.

The night they returned from the solicitor, he asked her one question. *Are you certain?*

She replied simply, "I am."

Trepidation had been her constant companion since she had accepted her inheritance. Her stomach was constantly in knots. Even so, she was determined to go through with it.

When she was alone in her room, she read over the paperwork in the folio Mr. Williams gave her. Once she accepted the inheritance and took possession of Ravenfell Manor, there was no going back. Since she was part of the bloodline, she was taking it as is, and there was no selling it. It was one of the clauses buried deep within the codicil that Mr. Williams hadn't pointed out.

The moment she read that, hot pinpricks danced up her spine.

But she was determined to do this thing on her own. She was set on forging her own path and becoming her own woman.

She gave her room one last glance before closing the door behind her and heading down the stairs. She had no intention of looking back. This was a place of sadness for her. Once she stepped foot onto Ravenfell estate, she would shed her sorrow and her mourning black and become the mistress she was meant to be.

Or so she hoped.

Aunt Eloise and Uncle Hubert waited at the front door. He, with his hat tucked under his arm and coat buttoned up. Her wringing her hands and her face pinched with worry. It was clear she was ready to launch into another diatribe about how inappropriate it was for Victoria, a single woman, to move to a country estate all alone.

With her small reticule in hand, Victoria steeled herself against the argument that was to come.

But Aunt Eloise remained mute as she halted in front of them, drawing in a steady breath. Her uncle gave her a warm, encouraging smile.

"Shall we?" He motioned toward the door.

Aunt Eloise made a whimpering sound. He gave her a warning glance. She pressed her lips together into a straight line, her hands still clenched.

"Do be careful, dear girl," she said. "I hope you'll keep in touch."

"I'll send a letter as soon as I'm settled," Victoria said with a reassuring smile. Though her stomach was still fluttering with nervous knots. She kissed her aunt's cheek. "Thank you for everything. It means the world to me you took me in."

The older woman's eyes grew misty. "We were glad to do it."

Though Victoria wondered about the truth of that.

She followed her uncle out the door and into the early morning sunshine. He intended to escort her to her new home to see her safely there. It would be a day's ride to Elderbloom and Ravenfell Manor. She had but one bag of her belongings packed on the carriage.

Once they were both settled, the carriage trotted away, leaving the busy city streets behind for the country. And, she hoped, a slower more peaceful way of life.

It was late in the day when they finally made it to the estate. Excitement followed by apprehension drummed through her as she peeked out the window. The carriage wheels crunched on the gravel drive as it made its way up the long road flanked by verdant green lawns perfectly kept.

The last of the evening sun touched upon the sprawling manor house that stood tall and imposing against the fading indigo sky. There, rising out of her memories, was Ravenfell Manor.

Its honey-colored stone walls reflected the dusky twilight, worn by time and ancient secrets. Ivy snaked across the timeworn walls toward the gables, and chimneys rose like pointed spires reaching for the sky. To one side, trees offered shade from the early summer sun. On the other side, a gate led to the grand garden that appeared to be in pristine condition. As if someone tended the fragrant blooms with loving care and attention.

The carriage came to a halt outside the grand entrance where the arched doorway was flanked by twin columns. Over the door, its pediment cracked as though it had once borne a family crest now lost to time. The tall paned windows reflected the twilight and—beyond—the faint glow of the interior that was less than welcoming.

The imposing structure stood silent, waiting, watching.

Victoria swallowed, a sudden lump of fear in her throat. Suddenly, her determination waned. It took everything in her not to tell her uncle to turn the carriage around and go back.

"Well, here we are," he said, trying to sound cheerful.

She hadn't realized he, too, was peering out the window watching as they approached the estate. He sat back, a smile plastered on his face as the footman opened the door and waited. Her uncle motioned toward the door to let her out first.

Hesitation pounded through her as she peered out the open carriage door.

No, she could do this. She *would* do this.

Picking up her reticule, she stepped out onto the gravel drive and moved aside to wait for her uncle. He followed her, pausing next to her, as the two of them gazed up at the house together. Her heart rammed against her chest. So hard it felt as though her ribs vibrated.

"Are you certain about this, dear?" he asked, his voice soft and full of concern.

She swallowed hard, her mouth suddenly dry. All she could do was nod.

He sucked in a deep breath, expelled it. "Very well, then."

Her uncle stepped toward the door and lifted his hand to knock when it cracked open. The hinges groaned with the effort as it slowly swung wide. A man stepped through the threshold into the gloom, his obsidian eyes landing on her with a curious glint—yet sharp and assessing. He already knew who she was and why she was there.

He was tall, dressed in a dark gray coat clinging to his broad shoulders, the fabric dulled by time and wear. His hair was black as crow feathers, curling slightly at the collar and around his ears, touched with a silver streak at the temples.

Angular features hosted high cheekbones, a straight, thin nose, and thin lips carved into a permanent grimace. And though he had the silver streaks at his temples, he had no wrinkles to speak of and looked as young as Victoria herself.

There was something unearthly about him. Not in the way of ghosts, but of someone who had once been alive and had not quite finished the job.

His head inclined as he looked at her with those black eyes, his gaze unreadable.

"You must be the new mistress," he said. His voice was low and smooth. Silky. Like chocolate. "You're earlier than expected."

He moved aside and motioned for them to come inside. Not a very welcome invitation, for she sensed his cold stiffness. Victoria, clutching her reticule in her gloved hands, took her first step through the threshold and into the grand foyer of the manor house. Her uncle followed, keeping close behind her as the man closed the door with another groan of hinges. It plunged the foyer into shadowy darkness.

She had never thought to be here again, yet the moment she stepped inside, it was as if time stood still. Everything was exactly how she remembered it. Impossibly unchanged.

The marble flooring, veined with silver and onyx, stretched beneath her feet. The grand staircase curved upward in a sweeping arch, the balustrade carved with floral vines. To the right, the old grandfather clock stood in its alcove, its slow tick echoing through the silence. Above her, the chandelier with its crystals that once shone brightly were now smudged by dust.

Beyond that, she caught a glimpse of the parlor, where the baby grand piano still sat in dignified silence. The instrument's lacquered black curve was reflected in the gilded mirrored walls, though the mirror's surface had aged. They were now dulled and veined with hairline cracks like a spider's web of memory. Dust shimmered in the slanted afternoon light from the windows on the opposite of the room.

It smelled faintly of lavender with a hint of stale air and something like old paper and extinguished candle smoke.

And it was hers.

The man stood to the side, eyeing her and her uncle as though waiting for her to speak.

"And you are?" She spoke in a weak and tremulous whisper, and then immediately cursed herself for sounding so frail.

"Gabriel Allward, miss. The caretaker of this estate." He gave her a half-bow, as though it was expected but he didn't mean it.

Her uncle stepped around her and offered his hand. "And I'm Hubert Pembroke, her uncle on her mother's side."

Gabriel's black eyes drifted to him, giving him a cool once-over. With some reluctance, he took his hand and shook it once, then released him.

"Good of you to travel with her. Will you be staying the night?" He sounded a bit agitated at the thought her uncle would, in fact, be staying.

"I—" he began.

"It's far too late for you to return, uncle. I'm sure we can find a guest bedroom for you." Her gaze slid to Gabriel. "Can't we?"

He gave a thin-lipped smile of annoyance. "Of course, miss." Then to her uncle, "Your horse can be stabled and cared for until the morning when you make your return journey."

But her uncle's brows had drawn together. His eyes were lit with suspicions. "Where is the rest of the staff?"

"I'm afraid there hasn't been staff here in many years, sir. I'm the only one."

Victoria sucked in a gasp. "You? Only you?"

"Yes, miss. There hasn't been a need to keep Ravenfell fully staffed with just me here." He smiled again, though it didn't reach his eyes.

"Seems odd you'd stay on," Uncle Hubert said.

Gabriel's smile faltered, though his posture remained perfectly composed. "Odd, perhaps. But I made a promise to stay. A promise I intend to keep." His gaze flicked briefly to Victoria. "Ravenfell doesn't take kindly to abandonment. Someone had to remain."

There was a subtle weight to his words. She wasn't sure what it was she sensed, but it went beyond duty and obligation.

Disconcerting silence settled between them. Uncle Hubert gave a quiet snort of disapproval, which was not like him at all. He was normally passive and taciturn. She ignored him as a prickling sensation skipped up her spine and paused with a cold tingling sensation at the nape of her neck. Like icy invisible fingers brushing across her skin.

Yes, someone had to remain.

The words bloomed over her in a roughened whisper but when she looked at the men in the foyer, neither had spoken.

There was something familiar about that voice and a memory resurfaced, sharp and quick like a flash of lightning. A little girl's voice telling her *don't be afraid,* and the haunting tune of the piano played by no one. Phantom footsteps on the landing. Her heart thudded, pounding a hard, erratic beat.

"Miss?" Gabriel's voice broke through her thoughts.

She looked up. His eyes held hers. Dark. Steady. Waiting.

Searching.

Questioning.

In that moment, she knew two things.

One, this man was not lying.

Two, he was waiting for her.

The grandfather clock chiming jarred her, making her jump. She put a hand to her head and rubbed, hoping to scour away whatever chilling feeling she had pulsing through her.

"Are you well?" he asked.

"I'm...fine. Just a little tired from the trip." She managed a smile.

"Then I should see you to your rooms. Would you care to dine this evening?" he asked.

She looked to her uncle for the answer. Perhaps he sensed her unease when he reached for her, taking her by the elbow.

"No, thank you, Mr. Allward. We dined in town before we arrived," Uncle Hubert said, taking charge.

For that, she was grateful.

"Gabriel, please. I must insist. Do you have bags?" he asked.

"In the carriage," Uncle Hubert replied.

"Very good, sir."

He gave a sharp nod as he headed back toward the door and pulled it open. Again, with the groan of hinges. As he exited the manor to see to the bags, her uncle turned to her. He had a pinched expression, one that was difficult to read.

He lowered his voice so only she heard his rushed words. "Victoria, darling, you don't have to do this. You aren't obligated to stay here. I can help you sell the place if you—"

"I'm staying," she said, cutting him off.

Because the thought of returning to Crown Hollow, under the care of her aunt, sent a pang of panic through her. She would much rather take her chances here, in this strange manor, than return to the city.

Her determination to be independent could be her undoing.

"I'll stay the night to make sure you get settled. Perhaps even stay through tomorrow night."

He cut a glance toward the open door where Gabriel retrieved the two suitcases. It was clear he didn't trust the man. Perhaps she didn't, either.

"I don't think that's necessary," she said. "Besides, I have to learn how to run the estate at some point. I'll hire more staff if that will make you feel better."

"It would, yes," he said with a definitive nod.

Gabriel returned carrying both their bags. "If you'll follow me, I'll show you to your rooms."

He started up the grand staircase.

She and her uncle exchanged a glance. His, wary. Hers, nervous. Together, they followed the caretaker up the stairs.

Chapter 3

The moment Gabriel opened the door to see Victoria Ravenwood bathed in the last breath of the waning evening, his heart jolted.

She was here. She had returned.

Her upturned face caught the last rays of the fading sun, highlighting her golden skin. It was hard not to notice the smattering of freckles across the bridge of her nose and upper cheeks. Or the way her hazel eyes shined with curiosity, a little fear, and perhaps a little recognition. Or the way golden strands gleamed in her perfectly coifed chestnut hair.

His pulse pounded.

This woman, this Victoria Ravenwood, was not the little girl he remembered. No. She'd grown into a vibrant, beautiful woman. There was something warm and gentle about her that was undeniable. Something that made his senses shift and take notice. He feared if she remained here, that vibrancy would dull and her light would be snuffed out.

He refused to acknowledge the sudden shift in his senses. The unwelcome pull toward the beautiful young heiress standing in his foyer.

Did she know what she stepped into when she came to Ravenfell Manor?

No, likely not. How had this come to pass? Surely, had her parents lived, they'd have never let her come here alone.

He remembered her as a child. But now she was a woman. Grown into a young lady of beauty and grace. And far too naïve to be the mistress of Ravenfell. She was never meant to return and yet, there she was, looking at him with a sense of familiarity as though she remembered him, as though she *saw* him for who and what he was. And that hope was the worst of it.

He banished that hope immediately. Locked it away in the deep, dark recesses of his heart in the same place he'd buried all the other feelings. Where it would starve, silent and unseen.

Now, Gabriel led the new mistress up the stairs to her room, his feet slow and methodical. The house, he knew, was listening. Watching.

Irritation clawed through him at the sight of the uncle. He wanted him gone, forthwith. He wanted him to return to wherever he came from and, if had any sense at all, he'd take Miss Ravenwood with him. She didn't belong here. She was far too delicate a flower for the sinister halls of the manor.

But the gentlemen in him refused to turn either of them away. And so, he led the uncle to his own room, handing off his bag and allowing him to settle. The man hovered in the doorway with concern gleaming in his bright eyes as he looked at Victoria.

"Good night, uncle," she said, her tone clipped. As though she was ready to be done with him and everything for the evening.

He gave a nod. "Good night, Victoria."

Then his gaze skipped to Gabriel. For a moment, Gabriel thought he saw a warning in the depths of the man's eyes. But then Pembroke gave a slight bow and shut the door with a snap, leaving the two of them alone in the hallway.

"Your room is just there." Gabriel pointed to the other end of the hall.

She nodded, saying nothing, allowing him to continue to carry her bag. He wondered, then, if there would be more bags arriving on the morrow. Trunks of dresses, hats, and shoes no doubt.

"Will your other things be arriving soon?" he asked, his voice loud in the quietness of the hallway.

"My other things?" she asked, her dark brows drawing together in question.

"Your trunks," he explained.

"Oh." She said the word on a breath. "I have no other things."

Surprise etched through him. He focused on the other end of the hall, the weight of her one bag suddenly heavy in his hand. She only had the one? Nothing more? He slid her a sideways glance wondering what happened to her. Wondering why she had the one bag. He refrained from asking, for he knew it wasn't his place to pry.

So, he said nothing as he picked up the pace to her room, his polished shoes making a clip-clip sound on the wood planks.

At the door, he paused for her to catch up. When she was close—too close for his comfort—he turned the knob and swung it open. He waited for her to step inside first, but she didn't. She hesitated in the threshold, peering inside the room with her hands tightly clenching the handle of her reticule.

"This is...my room?" Her voice was soft, full of wonder tinged with apprehension.

"Yes," he said his voice succinct.

When she did not move into the room, he stepped inside and placed her bag on the chair nearest the bed.

Finally, she took a step and gazed around with wide-eyed innocence that sent a sharp pang through his chest. Why did she have to look at it like that? Like the world was still full of beauty? Like this room was a gift?

Of course, she did. She likely hadn't seen one like it before.

It was palatial by most standards. The far wall held towering windows covered by thick brocade draperies that blocked the sun when they were pulled together. The heavy drapes were drawn aside, leaving only gossamer sheers to veil the tall windows, now tinted with dusk. In the morning, sunlight would spill through the gauze and slash across the hardwood floor and its thick, jewel-toned rug. Before the windows, a balloon-backed chair and a fainting couch in muted embossed damask sat in a quiet arrangement.

A fireplace, now dormant, was on the wall across from the large four-poster bed draped in velvet curtains. The marble mantle was bare. No portraits, no keepsakes. Just emptiness where memories should have been.

Next to the bed, on either side, a mahogany side table. A brass candelabra on each dulled by age. And finally, a mahogany armoire, ornately carved, on the same wall as the hearth.

Gabriel stood beyond the doorway, uneasy with how alive the room felt now that she was in it. Ravenfell had not been lived in for a long, long time. And yet, he feared it might remember how.

When she'd taken in the full expanse of the room, she turned to him. A blush crept into her cheeks as she caught his gaze still fixed on her. He hadn't looked away once. He should have looked away. It would've been polite. Safer. But he couldn't.

"I hope you find it to your liking," he said at last.

"Yes, thank you."

"I'm glad. If you need anything, use the bellpull."

He backed out of the room as she nodded. With his hand on the knob, he gave her one last glance before stepping out and closing the door. He paused outside her room for a long moment and waited. Listening. The silence pressed in. The only sound was that of his labored breathing and the roar of his pulse in his ears.

He had to step away. He had to return to his own space.

As he turned for the stairs, he noticed it. Fog curled low through the corridor like smoke from an unseen fire. The house was stirring.

When the door shut behind Gabriel, Victoria remained rooted in place in the middle of the room. She had never been in something so grand. She didn't recognize the space and couldn't even recall where her childhood room was. As though the house had shifted in her absence.

Gabriel's innocent question about the rest of her trunks conjured unwanted, raw memories to surface. The fire. The smoke. *Her parents.* Gone. Everything she owned burned with them. Life as she knew it, gone up in flames.

The only clothes she managed to bring with her were the ones packed in the case. A few gowns—one of those her mourning gown. No hats to speak of. A pair of shoes and gloves, which she wore. Though she doubted she'd need ball gowns or any other finery here in the isolated country.

It wasn't as though she'd have a season, like she'd hoped.

A chill permeated the room. She clutched her elbows and eyed the hearth, blackened from use. No fire resided there now. She should have asked Gabriel to start one before he left.

No matter.

At the armoire, she pulled open the door. Inside, on the top shelf, an extra blanket. Nothing else. It smelled faintly of dust, old wood, and non-use. Unpacking and hanging her gowns seemed rather ludicrous, so she left them for now and moved to the darkened windows.

Pushing aside the gossamer curtain, she peered out. Full on darkness pressed against the window panes. The full moon overhead cast a blue-white illumination over the perfect lawn, making it glisten. Beyond that, nothing but shadows and shapes.

She heaved a sigh as she let the curtain fall back into place.

"Well, then," she murmured. "I suppose this is home now, isn't it?"

She said it to no one but herself. The air thickened. A soft creak echoed through the rafters. The room shifted as though hearing her and agreeing. The air around where she stood turned suddenly icy, her arms pricking under the sleeves of her gown. The hair on the back of her neck stood on end.

She wasn't alone. She knew that without knowing how. A shudder went through her.

Shoving those thoughts away, she scurried to the bed where she kicked off her shoes, removed her gloves, tossing them on the bedside table, and quickly shucked her dress. Wearing nothing but her shift, she pulled back the coverlet and slid underneath the blankets, pulling them up to her chin. She left every candle burning in the hopes it would ward off whatever phantom lurked within the confines of her room.

Her wide eyes skipped from the cold fireplace to the windows to the armoire. Whatever she sensed, though, was gone.

Perhaps her tired mind was doing nothing but playing tricks on her. It was a long day, after all. She needed rest. In the morning sun, everything would look different.

She hoped.

She had to.

Because the dark was listening.

Chapter 4

Morning pressed against her closed eyelids. When she blinked open her eyes, she was momentarily disoriented as she tried to recall where she was.

Next to the bed, the candles had burned down to a nub and were snuffed out. Across from her, a cheerful fire flickered in the hearth. She sat up, pushing her fingers through her tangled hair as she tipped her head to the side in wonder.

Perhaps Gabriel had come into the room earlier that morning to light the fire. She never heard him if he did. She smiled, happy to have the warmth permeating the room.

Just as she suspected, everything looked better in the light of day. Brighter. Warmer. Happier. She shoved aside the blankets and swung her legs off the side of the bed. Her shoes were still where she left them. Her dress a crumpled heap on the floor.

A chuckle rose through her at her silly, paranoid behavior. Her imagination ran wild with thoughts of apparitions. It was nothing more than nerves in her new home.

She dressed quickly, preferring to leave her hair down but pulling it back at the nape and tying with a ribbon. After she slipped on her shoes, she headed out of her room and paused in the hallway to take it in.

The wood-paneled walls were lined with old portraits. Likely of the Ravenwood line. People she didn't know. Above the portraits, a row of dust-smudged windows. There were two spots that were empty—the portraits were removed, leaving a faint faded outline. Filtered morning light pressed against the grime, trying hard to brighten the otherwise dull corridor. A well-worn runner went the length of the hall and down the stairs, which, she thought, was strange. She recalled hearing Gabriel's click-click of his shoes as he led her to her room.

Behind her, there was a row of closed doors leading to the west wing. Bedrooms, no doubt. She idly wondered just how many bedrooms were in this house. And which one belonged to Gabriel.

As soon as the thought came to her mind, she shoved it away. It would not do to think about where the strange caretaker's bedroom was in relation to hers. With his cool demeanor toward her, it was clear he was not happy about her sudden arrival.

She headed down the stairs, her fingers lightly trailing the wood balustrade intricately carved with vines. The runner, she noticed, continued from the top of the stairs to the bottom. When she stepped off the last tread, she paused, glanced back up as a strange sensation pounded through her.

Last night, there was no carpet runner.

Or perhaps she didn't recall since she was tired.

At any rate, the old rug needed to be replaced. She made a mental note of that as she continued on her way to the dining room.

The sound of piano music, faint and lilting, stopped her. She turned, peering into the silent, dark parlor where the baby grand remained untouched. The lid closed. The bench shoved under it.

She started to turn away but then heard it again. Quiet notes. Delicate and deliberate echoing through the hush of the foyer. As though someone played to a great crescendo. The music mournful and oddly familiar.

Curious, and before she made the conscious decision, she turned toward the sound and walked into the parlor.

The music stopped.

The ceiling rose high above. On one end, the baby grand piano in front of a pair of windows draped in heavy velvet to block out the sun.

Her heart thudded as she stepped into the room, the scent of rosewood and lilacs teasing her nose. Once beautiful, the glory of the room had faded. Opposite the piano, a walnut carved settee and matching chairs in a rich garnet velvet. A tarnished silver tray rested atop a lace-covered table in the corner. There were no other decorations. No pictures. No vases. No bric-à-brac. Even the gilded mirrors lining the wall, once vibrant, had lost their sheen.

Another look at the piano to see the keyboard cover was closed.

She could not have heard the music, could she?

"Miss Ravenwood, can I help you?"

Gabriel's voice startled her. She whirled to see him standing in the doorway as her heart jolted. He stood stiffly, his dark eyes looking at her with wariness.

"I-I thought…" Then she clamped her mouth closed, pressing her lips together. "No, thank you."

She hurried from the parlor, her skirts whispering around her ankles as she crossed the foyer and slipped into the dining room. Gabriel followed, his steps light but ever-present, like a shadow trailing just behind.

The room greeted her with cool formality. A long mahogany table dominated the space, polished to a dull gleam and flanked by ten high-backed chairs, their legs curved like talons and seats upholstered in worn burgundy brocade. The fabric, though faded in places, still bore the elegance of another age.

Heavy damask curtains framed tall windows that let in a slant of gray morning light, dust motes dancing like ash in the air. A crystal chandelier hung overhead, its pendants silent and still.

To one side, a rosewood sideboard displayed an unused tea service and a line of delicate china dishes—bone white with gilded edges—each set precisely as though awaiting a gathering long past. The silver gleamed, polished but untouched.

At the far end of the table, a modest breakfast was laid out. A covered dish of toast still warm, a stack of flaky scones wrapped in linen, and a cut-glass bowl of dark red jam glinting like garnet in the light.

The food looked inviting. The room did not.

Victoria hesitated, one hand lightly grazing the back of a chair. Though her uncle sat at the table reading his paper, the silence felt too thick for the early hour. As though the room was waiting for someone to fill its emptiness again and wasn't sure yet how it felt about her.

When she entered, he glanced up and gave her a warm smile in greeting.

"Did you sleep well?" he asked.

Fatigue still pounded through her as she took the chair opposite him. Gabriel kept to the fringes of the room, waiting for her to make a request.

Discomfort shifted through her with his constant presence.

"Well enough," she replied. "You?"

"My room was delightful." He folded the newspaper and set it aside, then lifted the napkin to his mouth in a practiced motion. "Well, my dear. What do you propose we do with the day? You are mistress now. Time to make Ravenfell yours."

Gabriel was at her side then, holding a teapot. The scent of bergamot wafted to her nose. "Tea?"

She nodded as she answered her uncle. "We, uncle? Are you planning to stay then?"

Her uncle's gaze slid to Gabriel as he poured the tea, then straightened. "I thought I might for another day or so."

Uncle Hubert was wary of Gabriel. He wasn't ready to leave her alone with him. She dropped a lump of sugar in her cup and stirred.

"I suppose a tour would be wise. I don't remember much of the place and I ought to know what shape it's truly in."

Gabriel offered her the plate of scones still wrapped in linen. She waved it off.

"A tour is a grand idea," Uncle Hubert said, far too cheerful for the cheerless room.

"I shall be glad to guide you, Miss Ravenwood," Gabriel said in a quiet voice. Then, after the faintest pause, added, "And you, too, Mr. Pembroke."

She took a sip of tea, then replaced the cup and rose. "Shall we go now, then?"

Gabriel lifted a dark brow, his voice even. "Now, miss?"

"Why wait? I've quite lost my appetite." In fact, the smell of the meager breakfast made her already knotted stomach queasy. "I also would like to meet any other staff members who live here."

"Other staff members, miss?" He sounded quite confused.

"Yes. I'd like to thank whoever laid the fire in my hearth this morning. Unless that was you?"

He froze, his expression still and flat. "Not me, miss. And there are no other staff members in residence."

Victoria blinked.

A ripple of unease crawled over her skin, but she forced a small, dismissive smile. "Well, perhaps I was mistaken. It was warm when I woke, that's all."

But even as she said it, her thoughts tangled. She hadn't imagined the faint glow in the hearth or the comforting crackle of dying embers. And yet Gabriel's expression remained unreadable.

Her grip firmed on the chair's edge.

Perhaps it was lit the night before. Perhaps the stone simply held the heat. Perhaps—

No. She wasn't mistaken, nor would she let shadows chase her mind so soon. Not on her first day.

"Shall we begin?" With deliberate steps, she headed toward the dining room doorway.

Uncle Hubert was on his feet at once, folding the newspaper under one arm and trailing her out. His movements were brisk, but there was something in the way he glanced at Gabriel. A flicker of suspicion.

Behind them, Gabriel followed without a word.

A sort of uneasiness pierced the room as they crossed the threshold. Uneasiness between the three of them.

Once she was out of the dining room, Gabriel passed her. Her uncle moved to walk next to her. Victoria's shoes whispered over the floor as they headed back into the foyer. Her eyes flicked instinctively toward the grand staircase, and then upward where the chandeliers overhead stirred ever so slightly, though no draft touched her skin.

That prickling sensation was back, creeping up her spine. But she ignored it and kept moving, following Gabriel up the stairs.

"I suggest we begin in the east wing," Gabriel said at last, his voice soft but certain.

"How about the west wing?" she suggested, thinking of the row of closed doors.

"The east is a much better place to start, through the west does hold most of the older rooms. Those still untouched."

"Untouched?" she asked.

He gave the faintest nod. "Some haven't been opened in years."

Uncle Hubert cleared his throat. "And why is that, Mr. Allward?"

Gabriel's gaze didn't waver. "Some doors are better left closed, sir."

A heavy silence settled around them. Then Victoria turned away and pressed forward.

"Let's open them anyway," she said.

Apprehension shifted through his eyes. "But the east wing—"

"I insist," she said with a forced smile.

"As you wish, miss."

At the top of the stairs, they turned right instead of left like they had the night before. They headed down a long, dimly lit corridor where it seemed the candles in the sconces were unable to push back the shadows creeping along the walls. There were no windows here, either. Nothing to give any sort of light to press back the gloom.

Victoria didn't want to admit how dreadful this wing felt. Not only dreadful, but oppressive. As though some great tragedy had played out here. A faint whisper tickled her ear, and she thought, for a moment, it was a woman's voice.

Somehow, she managed to not react. Instead, she clenched her hands into tight fists at her sides, that sickly feeling creeping up to her throat and lodging there. Gabriel paused midway and turned to face them. The moment he did, the ominous presence she sensed was chased away.

"This is the west wing. Nothing but dusty bedrooms that haven't been used in years." He motioned to the closed doors on either side of the hall.

"I'd like to see them," she insisted, though she hadn't a clue why.

Again, he gave her that arched brow look. "All of them?"

"Yes, if you please."

With a curt nod, Gabriel reached for the door nearest him to his right. He pushed open the door, letting it *thunk* back against the wall into the room. No light spilled out.

Why she expected that, she did not know. She expelled a shaky breath as she approached the open threshold and paused there to peer inside.

A cold hearth sat unused and dark. Heavy drapes blocked out the one window. The bed was covered with a frilly pale coverlet. Across from it, a dressing table and armoire. The hardwood floor creaked as she took a step inside. There was no rug here to muffle the sound. The air was colder here.

She looked around and slowly realized this was a child's room.

She had never seen this room before. Of that, she was certain. Why did the air feel so heavy?

Victoria stepped back into the hall, backing out of the room. Her uncle and Gabriel remained where they were. Neither had spoken. When she was back in the hall, Gabriel reached for the knob and pulled the door shut, sealing it in silence once more.

"Shall we continue?" he asked.

One glance down the shadowed hallway had her shaking her head. "That's enough for now, I should think. Perhaps after luncheon we can look at the ledgers." She hooked her arm with her uncle's. "How about we take a stroll outside, uncle? I feel as though I need a bit of fresh air."

"Grand idea, my dear."

He didn't argue the point as he turned her away from Gabriel and headed for the stairs.

CHAPTER 5

Victoria couldn't shake the feeling that crept over her since the moment she stepped into the house. She chewed her lower lip as she and her uncle headed down the stairs and to the front door.

The hearth that seemingly lit itself. The phantom piano playing. The cold drafts. The strange sensations she sensed in that child's room.

Was it hers when she was little? She didn't recall. Perhaps it belonged to someone else in the family. Which got her to wondering how long Ravenfell manor had been in the family. Her father had inherited it from his father. But how many generations had lived here?

Her uncle released her arm to open the door for her and step aside. When she was out in the warm morning light, he followed. She headed toward the gardens where the sweet scent of the fully bloomed roses beckoned.

"My dear, are you well?" her uncle asked as he fell in step with her.

She took the footpath from the side of the house through the garden gate, her shoes crunching lightly on the gravel. "Yes."

"You seem..." He paused, searching for the words.

She stopped at a rosebush with full, pink blooms to sniff them. Their sweet scent made her close her eyes and smile.

"For the state the manor house is in, this garden is certainly well maintained," her uncle said. He glanced around at the blooming flowers.

"Yes," she agreed, releasing the flower and glancing up at the foreboding house.

Truthfully, it wasn't in all that bad of shape. The exterior could use some polishing, of course. The stone was dingy from dirt and moss. Grime crusted the windows. The shutters needed a good coat of paint. And who knew what shape the roof was in?

Her uncle placed a gentle hand on her arm. "Victoria, darling. You don't have to stay here if you don't want to."

Victoria hadn't shared with him the clause in the codicil that stated she must maintain ownership until her death when it was to be passed to the next of kin, or her child.

"Yes, I do, uncle."

She turned on the toe of her shoe and headed back up the path, going deeper into the garden. He followed.

"I want you to know, we'd be happy to have you back if you change your mind."

She suppressed a snort. The last thing she wanted to do was go back and live under the controlling thumb of her aunt. While the woman meant well, she was overbearing and highly opinionated. She was determined to see Victoria married off to someone—any-one—who would take her. Furthermore, she didn't want that woman scrutinizing her or telling her how to live her life.

"I do appreciate that, Uncle Hubert, but I'm determined to make a go of it here at Ravenfell."

As she said it, a raven flapped overhead. So close, in fact, she heard the flutter of its wings. It headed past her, disappearing over the stone wall at the back of the garden into the morning.

An omen.

Uncle Hubert matched her stride. She noticed then, with some chagrin, her legs burned from her hurry. She slowed, taking her time to examine the loveliness of the garden.

"I just don't want you to think you don't have a choice," he said.

Her dear uncle. Such a sweet man. He wanted the best for her, she could tell. And he worried about her being here alone with that caretaker. The caretaker who had dark eyes that seemed to watch her every move. Thinking of Gabriel sent a shiver through her.

There was something about him that made her a bit wary. A bit on edge. Something that told her he'd been here in Ravenfell far too long. She searched her childhood memories. Had he been here then? Skulking about the halls and keeping his watchful gaze on everything and everyone?

She couldn't recall.

Victoria halted at a bunch of lilacs, their scent wafting up toward her. They reminded her of her mother, who always preferred lilacs and lilies. A smile played at the corners of her mouth as she gazed at her uncle with his worried expression.

On impulse, she leaned over and kissed his cheek. "I thank you for that."

She started walking again. The morning sun was hot on the top of head and she wished she had a bonnet to shade her face from the bright rays.

"At least let me look over the ledgers with you and that man," he said.

Ever the banker. She grinned. "That man has a name, uncle."

"Yes, I know." He sniffed derision as though he was loathe to speak his name aloud. As though it might conjure the sudden presence of the man.

"I'm sure Gabriel can show me everything I need to know."

"I'm sure he can. However, I must insist."

She chuckled at his stern tone and relented. Her uncle was a banker, after all. He'd know if something was amiss in the ledgers. "All right, uncle. If you insist. We'll look at the ledgers together this afternoon. Perhaps while we have tea. Would that make you feel better?"

"You know it would, my dear." He paused at a particularly vibrant hydrangea, its petals a delicate shade of pale blue. "Your mother was an excellent gardener."

It sounded like an offhanded comment, but one that took Victoria by surprise. "My mother planted these?"

"The whole garden," he said with a fond smile. "Every path, every bloom. She had a gift. Won best in show three years running at the Elderbloom Flower Festival." He chuckled. "You should've seen her with a pair of shears and a sun hat. No one dared interrupt."

Victoria blinked. Somehow, she had never known. Her mother had always seemed like a ghost. Beautiful, remote, drifting from one social event to the next.

A weathered wooden bench sat several steps away. She resumed walking toward it, needing to sit with this new image of her mother. Her uncle followed and joined her, finding his place while she remained perched at the chair's edge.

"Tell me more about her," she said quietly. "Mother and Father traveled so much, I don't recall much about them."

Uncle Hubert folded his hands on his knees. His voice gentled.

"She loved the gardens. It was the only place she ever seemed at peace. But she was your father's wife, and that meant traveling. They were rarely still. He was a man of ambition. Always chasing diplomacy, deals, titles. She followed because she had to. She didn't always want to leave you behind."

Victoria's throat tightened. "Then why did she?"

Hubert hesitated. "Because that's what was expected. And because she thought you were safer in the city after they packed up and left Ravenfell. All the courts, the travel, the endless social engagements. Dragging you from place to place. She believed it would harden you. So, she left you with tutors and governesses and thought that was best."

A breeze stirred the hydrangeas, and for a moment, the garden seemed to sigh around them.

After they packed up and left Ravenfell. The words stuck in her mind.

She recalled with some unexpected clarity they left abruptly one night, never to return. Her mother had a ghostly look about her face as though she'd witnessed something she never wanted to see again or speak of. Her father, with his gruff exterior and stoic face, led them from the manor to a carriage that took them to their home in the city.

After that it was nonstop travel for them and seeing very little of her parents.

"She loved you, Victoria," he added. "But she was raised to keep love at a distance. Like your father. They both were."

"They may have loved me but I was not enough to keep them home." She placed her hands in her lap and scooted back, her gaze on the swaying flowers ahead.

It was quiet here in the garden. She quite understood why her mother would prefer it. There was solace in the soil and the blooms.

"Your father had his work."

"Work," she scoffed. "Social galas. Political events. Foreign courts. And for what? What did that get them?"

She wondered if her mother had whispered her regrets into the flower beds. If she'd ever looked at the train schedule and considered staying behind, just once.

"Abner lived a prestigious life. Your mother had to attend with him on those social events to show the world he was a man of honor and respect. They were both shaped by duty, not desire. That's a hard thing to break from even for love."

Victoria lowered her gaze to her lap, her hands twisting together. "Do you think she was happy, uncle?"

Her uncle didn't answer right away. When she looked up, he was watching the blooms blow in the faint breeze, as though the flowers might speak before he could.

"I think," he said slowly, "she was waiting for the day she could stay."

Victoria nodded, the silence folding in around them once more.

"Then perhaps," she said quietly, "it's time someone stayed."

CHAPTER 6

T he lady and her uncle returned from their garden walk. Her cheeks were flushed, but she looked happy. Such joy had not echoed through these dark, desolate halls in quite some time. She announced she would retire to her room for a rest and wished to look over the ledgers during afternoon tea.

Gabriel frowned as he watched her disappear up the curved staircase.

"I trust that's not an inconvenience for you?" came a voice behind him.

He stiffened. The voice jolted through him like a needle. He hadn't realized the man was standing there, watching him watch her.

Gabriel turned slowly, his jaw tight and his gaze unreadable. "Not at all, sir."

Hubert said nothing more. He ascended the stairs for his own afternoon rest.

Gabriel's fists clenched at his sides. He disliked the man's presence drifting through his halls, peering at him with those beady, suspicious eyes. He did not seem in any hurry to leave the manor and return to his city life.

He sensed the shift in the surrounding air. He exhaled, and his breath misted in the air, curling like smoke. The scent of lilacs and roses followed, faint but unmistakable. He froze.

You should be rid of him. And soon. Before something dreadful happens.

The voice, soft, lilting, disembodied, whispered at his ear. He hadn't heard her in years. And yet...there she was.

It wasn't merely a warning. It was a promise.

The malevolent force that haunted Ravenfell had been dormant for many long years. But from the moment Miss Ravenwood arrived with her uncle in tow things began to stir. Shadows clung to the corners of the west wing. Cold patches settled in the child's room she had insisted on opening. Something unseen awakened.

And he knew it was *her*.

Stalking. Watching. Waiting.

"Please don't," he whispered. "He means no harm."

Doesn't he? the voice returned. *He doesn't trust you.*

Gabriel closed his eyes and expelled a slow breath. He didn't need the voice to tell him that. It was evident in Hubert Pembroke's glances, in the tight line of his jaw, the glint of suspicion in his eyes.

He'll want to see the ledgers. You cannot allow that.

"Go away," Gabriel snapped.

The scent drifted off with a chuckle. Then everything returned to normal.

Gabriel remained at the base of the stairs, rooted in place. The only sound was the steady tick of the grandfather clock and then, faintly, the tinkling of piano keys echoing from the parlor. Three soft notes, then silence.

Her way of signaling she was leaving. For now.

She would return. She always did.

He sighed. As much as he hated to admit it, she was right. Hubert Pembroke would want to see the ledgers.

His first order of business was to do what he could to conceal the truth.

He hurried from the foyer to the study tucked at the end of the corridor in the east wing on the first floor. He pushed open the dark-stained oak door and entered, preferring to leave the lamps unlit and use the faint light from the window instead.

He knew where he was headed and, anyway, the gloom suited him.

Inside, the stale, unused room smelled of old parchment, leather bindings, and the mineral oil used to polish the wood desk. Beneath that, though, the lingering scent of wood smoke and something older like tobacco permeated in the wainscoting. Dust settled into the velvet curtains on the window.

Bookcases lined the walls from floor to ceiling, crammed full of old books that were in every shape and binding. Some with cracked leather covers. Others with fraying cloth. Most were ledgers, estate records, and obscure volumes on local law and plant lore. A narrow ladder rested against one shelf, though Gabriel didn't need to use it. He'd memorized the layout of this room.

The mahogany desk stood before the cold, silent hearth. A monstrosity that once hosted the lord of the manor. Though the wood had been polished years ago, the scent remained despite its dull sheen. One corner was cluttered with sealing wax, quills, stacks of parchment that were unanswered letters and invitations from ages past. As though the former owner left them there with the intention of returning and answering them but never had.

The ledgers were locked inside the cabinet to the left of the desk. Not all of them. Only *those*. The ones that whispered secrets no one need hear.

As Gabriel knelt before the cabinet, a gust of cold brushed the back of his neck. The shadows in the corners shifted.

Lenore.

He reached for the key in his pocket, the one he kept on him at all times. With shaking fingers, he stuck it in the lock. Or tried. He missed once, twice, until he finally managed to slide it inside and twist.

Nevermore.

Her lilting voice brushed his ear, sending cold tingles erupting across his skin.

"Don't," he said, his voice hard and cold in warning.

Though what warning he could give her, he didn't know.

He pulled open the cabinet door and was greeted with dust and cobwebs. No one had been in this cabinet for years. Not since he'd hidden these away never to be seen again. Not since he'd tucked away the last pieces of Abner Ravenwood's investigation. Gabriel had hidden the journal deep inside, locked away with the hope it would never be found.

Now, with the looming threat of Hubert Pembroke and his banker's eye, he had to move the ledgers before they were discovered, before he was forced to show them everything.

These were the real ones. Not the tidy duplicate residing in the uppermost drawer of the desk. The one meant for review by a sharp-eyed banker. As he reached inside, his hand brushed over the leather-bound journal, still tied. He pushed it aside and grabbed the first ledger. This one was bound in cracked, blackened leather. He lifted it with care. Mold and mildew clung to the damp cover from being too long in the dark.

Lenore was stirring again.

His first intent was to get them out, all of them. He'd hide them somewhere else. The priest hole beneath the wine cellar, perhaps. Or the root cellar where no rat dared scurry. He pulled out the second. As he reached for the final one, the heaviest one with his sins written there, he noticed a corner sticking out. As though the page had been disturbed by someone or something.

With a shaking hand, he opened it to that page and froze. His throat tightened.

Fresh ink was penned in the center. Written there was one familiar name.

Victoria Ravenwood

With trembling fingers, he closed it with a muffled snap. His stomach dropped.

He recognized the familiar looping script of a woman long dead. He knew all too well what was written within those pages. He dropped the books to the floor, closed and locked the cabinet. Snatching up the books, he staggered to his feet.

If her name was scrawled there on the page, then there must be more to it. More he had yet to see or read. Did he dare?

He was certain he had to know. Hiding them in the root cellar would not do. He needed to read them so to prepare for what may come. Because, above all, he needed to protect Victoria.

You cannot stop it. No matter what you do.

Ignoring the taunt, Gabriel tucked the books under his arm and turned to go, when he heard a creak outside the door. He halted, his heart ramming hard in chest as he waited.

Victoria appeared in the open doorway.

As if her name in the book conjured her.

He couldn't let her see this. He couldn't let anyone see this. Her name burned behind his eyes like a brand and he didn't know what it meant. Not yet.

Her eyes were wide and round as her gaze fixed on the bundle under his arms.

"Oh," she said on a breath. "I thought I heard someone in here. Are those the ledgers?"

Gabriel forced a smile. "Old estate records. I ran across them while I was gathering the books for you. They're from decades ago, long before your parents' time. Most are riddled with mold and rot. I thought it best to move them somewhere drier before they completely fall apart."

She shifted, her gaze flickering from his face to the bundle under his arms. "May I see them?"

He chucked lightly. Too lightly. "Truly, there's nothing of interest. Inventory lists. Grain tallies. Ledgers from before Ravenfell was even Ravenfell. I promise, the more relevant books are in far better condition."

He hustled by her, leaving her standing in the doorway. With his heart in his throat, he managed to escape the study and further scrutiny by the lovely Victoria Ravenwood. Once he stashed these books, he'd return to grab the legitimate ones and meet her and her uncle in the parlor for tea.

A simple plan. And it would take all his calm to pull it off.

CHAPTER 7

Victoria watched Gabriel rush from the room as though something chased him. It was truly odd. But she pushed it out of her mind as she entered the room. No candles burned. Nor was there the telltale sign they had just been snuffed. He was in here in the dark? Why?

Again, odd.

But then, the caretaker was odd. Well, more like cold and aloof. She wasn't sure why she ended up at the study. She was restless after the garden walk and unable to stay in her room.

With her hands clasped behind her back, she perused the room. The bookshelves were lined with old books that smelled like dust, time, and forgotten things. The desk was cluttered with yellowed papers that appeared to be from another age. A quick glance down the parchment on top revealed an invitation to a ball decades ago.

Lifting the creased parchment, she searched for an address, but there was none. She wondered if this was something her parents were invited to and, clearly, did not attend. The date was right before the time they left Ravenfell.

Replacing it, she continued her tour of the room. Here, like the other rooms, there were no personal effects. No decorations. Nothing to indicate someone lived here and collected things.

Unbidden, a memory surfaced of being in this room when it was more cheerful, the fireplace was lit with a warm fire, and her mother was curled on one of the chairs with a book in her hand. Her father sat at the desk muttering about the state of the world. While she, Victoria, sat on the floor by the fire playing with her favorite doll in a blue gingham dress with a faded cloth face.

Something in the room shifted. A hint of lilacs and smoke tugged her mind backward until, as a child, she was once again sitting before the hearth.

The girl with blonde, glossy curls took a seat across from her, her legs crossed as she peered at her with wide blue eyes. Her face was pale, her eyes hollow with dark slashes under them. But Victoria was happy to have a playmate.

"Hello," she said to the girl. "What's your name?"

"Lily. What's yours?"

"I'm Victoria. Victoria Marie Ravenwood. I have three names. Do you?"

"No."

Victoria patted the hair of her doll, then cradled it against her chest while the other girl, Lily, looked on.

"I like your doll's blue dress. Can I play with it?" Lily asked.

"I don't have any dolls. My father took them all away."

"That's mean. Why did he do that?"

Victoria's mother was suddenly on her feet, standing near her. Her father had stopped shuffling papers at the desk to gape at her.

"Victoria, honey, who are you talking to?" her father asked, his tone gentle.

"Lily," she replied. "She wants to play with my doll."

Her mother emitted a strangled gasp. "Abner, do something."

"Take her out of here," her father said.

Victoria looked up at her mother, whose face was pinched with worry and a hint of fear. She reached a hand down to her.

"Come, Victoria, darling."

"But—"

"Do as your mother says," her father said, his voice sharp.

As Victoria reached for her mother's hand, she looked back to where Lily was sitting. But the girl was gone.

Victoria's foot caught on a wrinkle in the rug as she jerked back from the desk. Her pulse hammered in her ears. The chill on her skin wasn't imagined. It spread across her arms like icy fingers, as if something followed her out of the long-buried memory.

She pressed a hand to her chest. No one else had seen Lily. And yet...she remembered the blue eyes, her ashen face. The way her mother's voice shook and her father's stern, worried expression. Could it have been real? Could it still be?

It must have been something because her parents insisted they leave the study at that moment. Her mother took her out, her father following. He closed the door with a snap.

It was hard to shake the feeling coating her skin, though. Did her parents leave Ravenfell because they thought it was...haunted? That seemed absurd.

A coldness seeped into her bones then as she peered around the shadowy room. Her breath plumed. She backed toward the door as her gaze scanned the furniture. She saw nothing and no one. But she had the distinct feeling she was being watched.

Finally, she turned and fled the study.

And ran right into Gabriel. She crashed into his tall form. He reached up, grasped her arms to steady her. His grip on her arms was firm but careful, his gaze scanning her face. A hint of worry was there but something else. Fear? Recognition?

"Miss Ravenwood, are you all right?"

Victoria lifted her gaze to his, her heart a rapid flutter. She put on a smile. "Yes. My apologies. I didn't see you there."

"I gathered." He released her and stepped back. His gaze shifted to the open door behind her. "I was coming to retrieve the ledgers."

"Good. We can review them in the parlor."

"Now? I thought this afternoon with tea. Would you rather have luncheon first?"

"Oh. Yes, of course."

Without another word, she hurried around him and headed to the dining room. But her heart had not stopped racing. When she arrived, her uncle was already there.

"Ah, there you are, my dear. Did you have a nice rest?"

Clasping her shaking hands, she sat in one of the chairs. "Yes. You?"

"Are you certain? You look pale," he said.

She remained perfectly still, willing her heart to slow. "I'm fine." She punctuated that with a weak smile. "I'm quite famished."

Before her uncle could ask another question, Gabriel entered to serve them luncheon.

Later that afternoon, she and her uncle convened in the parlor. Moments later, Gabriel entered carrying a long, leather-bound book. He handed it over to her uncle.

"As you requested, sir."

Uncle Hubert gave a nod of thanks. Gabriel turned on the heel of his polished shoe and headed out of the parlor. Her uncle watched his departure, then looked her way. He looked as though he wanted to say something, but didn't as he flipped open the book.

"I hope you don't mind if I look this over first," he said.

"Not at all. I trust your judgement, uncle."

As he scanned the first page, Gabriel returned with the tea cart. He poured tea and served them both. Her uncle took his cup without looking up. When Gabriel extended the cup to her, she took it and met his gaze. His fingers brushed hers as she took the cup. A jolt skittered up her spine. He looked away too quickly. Why did that feel like guilt?

"I trust everything is in order?" Gabriel asked.

"How far back do these ledgers go?" her uncle asked without looking up.

"Several generations, I should think."

Her uncle flipped a page, running his finger down the length and making a *hmm* now and then. Then he took a sip of tea and closed the book.

"Everything appears to be in order," he announced, extending the book back to Gabriel.

Her uncle sounded almost disappointed by that. As though he were looking for some reason to accuse Gabriel of misappropriating funds or some other nefarious crime.

Gabriel stepped to her uncle and took the ledger from him. His glance slid to her as he held it.

"Would you like to take a look, Miss Ravenwood?"

She shook her head. "If my uncle says everything is in order, then that's good enough for me."

He nodded once. "Very well."

And then he left them alone. Victoria sipped her tea, peering at her uncle over the rim waiting for him to say something. He had a distant, strange look on his face as though he wasn't sure he was happy with the results of his audit.

"Uncle?"

"The estate hasn't had a full staff for quite some time," he said then. "You'll want to remedy that, I'm sure, now that you'll be living here full time."

She placed her cup and saucer on the table. "Uncle, you sound disappointed I'm staying."

He rose and moved to sit next to her. With his free hand, he took hers.

"I admit, I am sad you'll be so far from us in the city. However, I'm elated that you have this place and will be able to make a life of your own here." He squeezed her hand. "If you ever want to visit, please know you're always welcome."

"This sounds like goodbye, uncle."

A smile tipped the corners of his mouth. "For now. I expect to see you at holidays."

"Of course." She smiled back. "I'll miss you."

"And I will miss you. I've no doubt you'll do well here," he said.

He released her hand and rose, still holding the teacup. "Now, I suppose I'll go pack my bag. I'll be leaving in the morning."

She nodded. He dropped his cup on the cart as he exited. As she watched him go, she could not help the sense of foreboding that washed over her.

CHAPTER 8

That night, Victoria settled into her room. She yanked the blankets to her chin and huddled beneath them. The candles by her bedside guttered in the dark, throwing long, twitching shadows across the ceiling.

She told herself she wasn't afraid of the dark, but Ravenfell had a way of unmaking certainties. Every creak felt like a whisper. Every shadow, a warning. She laid there, staring at the ceiling, trying to make her eyes shut and go to sleep but everything in her told her to stay awake.

With a huff, she pushed away the blankets and sat up, swinging her legs over the side of the bed. She found her slippers and then rose, dragging her dressing gown off the foot of the bed and wrapping it around her shoulders. She a distraction to keep her mind occupied while she tried to sleep. She decided to go to the study and find something to read. Something dull that would put her right to sleep.

Snagging the candle off the bedside table, she exited her room and paused in the drafty hallway. A shiver went up her spine. It was cold, yes, but not the same chill she felt when she opened the child's room.

She headed for the stairs when something pulled at her, making her halt. Her gaze flickered to the west wing. The candle flame sputtered as if disturbed by a breath that wasn't there.

She didn't know why she turned right instead of left, only that something in her bones urged her to go. That same pull she'd felt earlier.

That wing of the house seemed to be in perpetual darkness with shadows curling and crawling along the floor and walls. Her footsteps, silent on the floor, took her down the hall, past the curved staircase and to the entrance to the west wing. She paused there, peering into the gloom.

Her heart throbbed as she gripped the candlestick tighter. What was she doing? She didn't need to go in there. She should turn back. Go down to the study and find a book to read.

But instead, she took another step toward the hallway and another and another, until she was standing in front of the door she'd opened earlier that day. Her shaking hand reached for the knob, but she pulled it back, clutching it against her chest.

Victoria turned away.

But as she did, she heard the faint whimper coming from behind the closed door.

She turned back, peered at the door, her heart now pounding a frantic beat. She stepped toward the door, wrapped her hand around the knob and twisted.

The moment the door swung open, the cold air slammed into her and wrapped around her like an icy winter breeze. As she stood in the doorway, she heard the soft sob of a young girl but there was no one in the room.

Even so, she took another step into the shadows, the candle flame flickering but not giving much light.

The room was exactly as it was earlier. Pale coverlet smoothed over the bed, dark drapes suffocating the only window, the armoire looming like a silent sentry in the corner. The room, though, was colder than before. Her breath fogged when she breathed out. The candle flickered violently, the flame nearly extinguished. She held her breath, her eyes fixed on the flame as it recovered and reignited.

A creak behind her. She spun, but nothing was there. The crying had stopped, but the shadows seemed to move. With her heart in her throat, she turned back intending to flee but something at the window caught her eye.

A glint of light.

From her candle.

She stepped closer, the floor beneath her felt ice cold as though it had not seen sunlight in years.

A mirror stood against the window. It hadn't been there before. In the glass, she saw herself, ghastly and pale, her white nightdress glowing like burial linen.

And behind her, a child.

Not beside her. Behind.

She turned so violently, she dropped the candle. It thumped against the floor and snuffed out, plunging her in total darkness.

She bent to pick it up. A breath like winter brushed across her cheek.

Then came the whisper, feathering against her skin. "You left me. Where did you go?"

Victoria jerked upright, stumbled backward, and crashed into the armoire with a thump. There was no one there, but she recognized that voice. With it came the weight of memory, bitter and sharp. A girl. A promise. A door shut too soon. Had she forgotten someone?

Another whisper, closer this time. "I waited for you to come back."

Then, a brush against her hand. A strangled whimper escaped her. She stood frozen, paralyzed by fear.

The cold vanished as quickly as it appeared and she was left standing there, huddled against the armoire, shivering in the dark. A quick glance at the window showed her there was no mirror there at all.

Without retrieving the candle, she fled the room, slamming the door closed. She ran to her room, her gown fluttering behind her. When she made it to her room, she closed and locked the door, backing up to the bed until her legs banged against it. She sank into the mattress, her eyes fixed on the door.

Her gut was coiled in tight knots as she glanced around the room.

Then she saw it. On the bedside table where her candle had been, a crushed lilac.

Victoria slept. She awoke to a knock on her door and a muffled voice calling her name through it. When she finally dragged herself from the depths of sleep, she sat up, yawned and realized the morning light pressed against the window.

"Victoria?" came the call again.

It was her uncle.

She shoved off the blankets and stood, realizing she was still in her dressing gown. Her slippers were discarded by the bed. When she'd returned to her room after the incident, she'd not bothered to remove her robe and instead climbed into bed, shivering under the covers until she finally managed to sleep.

"Coming," she called.

A quick look in the mirror of her dressing table revealed her disheveled appearance. Her hair was a mess of tangles. There were dark circles under her eyes. It was difficult not to see the fatigue lining her features.

She tied up her hair quickly and then hurried to the door, opening it a crack to see her uncle, fully dressed with his hat, standing in the hall.

"Still abed?" he asked, one brow raised. "You missed breakfast."

"What time is it?" Her heart lurched.

"Quarter to ten. You look exhausted." Concern flickered through his gaze as he looked her over. No doubt noticing she was still in her nightclothes.

She forced a smile. "I'm fine. Just tired. I didn't sleep well last night."

That was an understatement. Even when she did sleep, it was fitful and plagued with nightmares.

"The carriage is leaving to take me back to the city. I was hoping to see you before then." Disappointment creased his face.

"Give me a moment. I will be down to see you off. I'll meet you downstairs."

He nodded as she closed the door with a quick snap. She peered around the messy room, trying to pull herself together. Her gown was still discarded on the chair near the wardrobe. Her shoes left there. She ripped off the robe and hurried to the wardrobe to find something to wear. As she tugged out a pale yellow gown, she halted, realization pounding through her.

Once her uncle left for the city, she would be alone in this house with Gabriel.

Her breath hitched as she clutched the gown to her chest.

Did she dare remain here with him? With everything that happened last night—which she did not want to think about—she wasn't sure she *could* stay. Was she strong enough? Bold enough?

What choice did she have?

Return with her uncle to his brownstone in the city where her meddling aunt was determined to see her married off or...

She swallowed hard.

Or she could stay. Make a life here. For her mother, who had once found peace in these gardens. For the little girl who whispered through the walls. For herself, becoming the independent woman she dreamed of becoming since the moment the letter from the solicitor landed in her hands.

Breathing in deeply, she knew what she had to do. She was staying. And she had very little time to dress before her uncle departed. She tidied her hair, pulling it back and tying it with a silk ribbon. Then she dressed in the yellow gown, stuck her feet in her shoes, and headed down the stairs.

Her uncle waited in the foyer, his bag in hand. Gabriel was nowhere in sight, which was a relief. She dreaded facing him this morning, though she couldn't say why. Something about the previous night's events left her spooked to her core.

As she stepped down, she plastered on a bright smile, then hooked her arm in her uncle's.

"I'm sorry to see you go," she said. "Are you sure you can't stay longer?"

"I've been away from your aunt and the bank too long already." He patted her hand.

Gabriel appeared, silent and stealthy, already at the door. She startled when she saw him, though his face remained unemotional. She hadn't heard a footstep. Had he been there the whole time? Perhaps he was concealed within the shadows and she hadn't noticed him.

Uncle Hubert gave the man a polite nod as he headed out into the warm morning sunshine. There was something about the bright day that chased away all her fears and apprehension. The carriage waited on the gravel drive, its lacquered exterior shining brightly. Cheerfully. The driver sat perched on the seat holding the reins. The footman stood to the side waiting patiently for the arrival of her uncle.

Uncle Hubert seemed unbothered by the impatient look on both men's faces. When they were out of the house and closer to the carriage, he paused and turned to her.

"I do hope you fare well here, my dear. I don't want to worry about you," he said.

"There's nothing to worry about." Even as she said it, forcing a smile, a quiver of fear flickered through her. "I'll be fine here."

He cast a glance toward the garden. "I hope you'll hire a groundskeeper and a butler, at the very least."

"I plan to put out a solicitation as soon as I'm able."

"Good." He kissed her cheek. "Take care. And, Victoria, dear..." He paused, his eyes flicking back toward the house. "Please take care of yourself."

Something about the way he said it sent a chill through her. She wasn't sure what he was trying to tell her, but she sensed it was a warning somehow. As though he didn't quite trust Gabriel. And perhaps he didn't.

Perhaps *she* didn't, either, but she was here. As soon as she had the manor properly staffed, she'd find a way to dismiss the caretaker for good. She didn't need him skulking about the shadows, after all.

"Come see us when you can," Uncle Hubert said.

She nodded. "I promise."

Then he was stepping into the carriage. The footman closed the door, sealing him inside. Moments later, he was off. The carriage clattered down the gravel drive toward the road, leaving a cloud of dust in its wake and a sense of dread coiling through her gut.

CHAPTER 9

Victoria closed the front door behind her with a hollow click that echoed through the cavernous foyer. Dust veiled the floor in a thin film. Cobwebs draped from the corners like tattered lace, and the once-grand chandelier hung motionless above her. There seemed to be dust and cobwebs and neglect everywhere she looked.

Her uncle was right. This house, as proud and sprawling as it was, needed help. It needed life again.

She would start with staff.

But first, food.

She turned toward the dining room, her stomach hollow. Maybe some remnants of breakfast remained. But when she stepped through the archway, the long table was already cleared. Not a crumb in sight. The room was silent. A faint clink drifted from beyond.

She followed the sound to the kitchen.

The moment she pushed the door open, she halted. Surprise etched through her.

Gabriel stood at the sink, sleeves rolled to his elbows, rinsing the final teacup. He moved with quiet precision, his back to her, utterly unaware—or unconcerned—by her presence. He placed the cup on a cloth to dry and turned, finding her staring.

"Oh," she said, breath catching. "You've already cleared everything. I thought perhaps there was a cook I hadn't met yet."

He reached for a linen towel, dried his hands in smooth, practiced strokes, then met her gaze. His face, as always, was unreadable.

"There is no cook, Miss Ravenwood," he said simply. "I prepare what's necessary."

"You?" The word slipped out, tinged with disbelief. "You do all this yourself?"

That explained the dust. The disrepair. He was only one man. And this house—this estate—was far too much for one person to manage.

"It's part of my duties," he said, voice neutral, practiced.

She crossed her arms, gaze sweeping the room. Unlike the rest of Ravenfell, the kitchen was tidy. Counters gleamed. Copper pots hung in perfect rows above the stove. No splatters. No crumbs. No clutter. Every drawer and cabinet shut tight, everything in its place.

His place.

This was his domain.

And yet, he stood there like a statue. Towel clutched tightly in his hands. Eyes guarded. Walls so thick she'd need a chisel to get through them.

Was it that he didn't want her here? Or was that just who he was—distant, cold, unknowable?

Either way, if she didn't find a way to coexist with Gabriel Allward, her new life would be far lonelier than she'd imagined.

"I can't have you doing it all," she said, stepping farther into the room. "I intend to send out inquiries today. The house needs a proper staff. A cook, for sure. A housekeeper. A groundskeeper. Possibly a butler."

His jaw ticked. Barely. But she noticed.

"As you wish, Miss Ravenwood," he said, folding the towel with precision. "I'd be happy to deliver the letters on your behalf."

She arched a brow. "No need. I'll manage. A walk will do me good."

Something unreadable passed through his expression, then vanished as quickly as it came. "As you say."

She left the kitchen with a new sense of purpose and a touch of unease. The manor might not want her here, and Gabriel certainly wasn't going to make it easy.

But it was her house now.

And she would make it her own.

When she left the kitchen, Gabriel sagged against the sink. The quiet returned. But it wasn't comforting. Not anymore. He braced himself against the sink. The thought of strangers roaming the halls again, touching things best left untouched, made his skin crawl.

Apprehension swept through him at the thought of the lady hiring more staff. If she hired staff, where did that leave him? He was bound here. He could not leave, even if he wanted to. He knew, from experience, that would not go well. Ravenfell would not want that.

Nor would Lenore.

He hadn't sensed her presence all morning. A reprieve, he hoped. The moment new employees arrived, she would become ever present. Lingering in the shadows and doing her best to make life unbearable for everyone in the manor.

Himself included.

He hadn't had a chance to look over the ledgers he took from the study. But the fresh ink with Victoria's name haunted him. He suspected he knew what that meant, but he didn't want to admit it. He preferred not to think about the past.

And he certainly could not think about a future with the new mistress.

The scent of lilacs lingered, enveloping him. As though his thoughts conjured her. She was here.

You cannot allow her to hire staff.

His chest constricted. "Please, don't," he whispered. "She is the new mistress."

She's already disturbed the west wing more than once.

"She didn't mean to. She didn't know."

That doesn't matter. It didn't then. It doesn't now.

His mouth went dry as he turned to face the sink. His gaze fixed on the window over it, peering into the garden where the herbs swayed in the wind and the flowers fluttered against the breeze.

The days of serenity were over. His solitude was gone. And with that meant the return of Lenore and—

No. He wouldn't think of that now. He couldn't. The memory was too painful. He shoved the thoughts back down into the shadowed recesses of his mind. His eyes closed against the cheerful garden to push those dark thoughts back.

Darkness. Yes, he deserved to live in darkness for the rest of his miserable days for what he did. He deserved to be alone and forgotten.

Get rid of her. Or I will.

Lenore was gone leaving behind her dangerous threat.

He sagged against the sink, that tightness in his chest refusing to leave. There was no way to get rid of Victoria. Her determination to stay was written all over her face when she stood in the kitchen and announced her intention to hire more staff. He offered to take the letters for one reason only—to destroy them. He didn't have the heart to tell her no one would answer her advertisements, but she would find out soon enough. The rumors Ravenfell manor was cursed or haunted had swirled through the village for years.

But then, they weren't mere rumors, were they?

The manor *was* cursed and haunted. And only now that the new mistress was in residence did the shadows stir once again.

Which reminded him about the ledgers. Thinking of them once again, he flung down the dishtowel and headed out of the kitchen. He paused in the foyer, listening for any signs of life within the manor. Victoria was likely in the study writing her letters. If so, she would be there for a while.

Which would give him time to look at the ledgers undisturbed. He hurried up the stairs to his room at the far end of the hall in the east wing. He did his best to avoid the west wing whenever possible. Too many memories. Too much sadness.

And when Victoria forced him to open the door to the child's room, his heart cleaved in two.

At his room, he shoved open the door and closed it with a click. He'd hidden the ledgers under the dusty bed. Kneeling, he pulled them out, then sat back on his heels and stared down at the books.

Apprehension swept through him as he reached for the top one, his hand shaking. When he flipped it open, he halted. There was Victoria's name written in the blood-colored ink.

But below was a new line scrawled there.

Do not love her or she will take my place.

He slammed the book closed and shoved it back under the bed. He scrambled back to his feet and stumbled backward until his back smacked the closed bedroom door.

The warning was clear. The danger was present. And he was certain Lenore would make good on her threat.

Chapter 10

When Victoria finished her letters, she folded them and sealed them with wax. She decided to walk down to the village to post it to the Crown Hollow Tribune in the hopes of getting more response from interested parties, rather than solicit the local village. The second letter was to her aunt giving her an update on life in the estate, though she suspected her uncle would share that information upon his return.

Still, she felt it necessary to write the letter to let Aunt Eloise know all was well and not to worry about her. She kept the tone light and positive. She did not mention any of the strange happenings in the manor because she, herself, was not certain they had actually happened.

After she retrieved her hat and gloves, she headed out of the manor and down the gravel drive, the morning sun lifting her spirits. She had convinced herself the things she'd seen and experienced inside the old estate was nothing more than her imagination or perhaps the residue of a bad dream.

Her experience in the child's room never happened. Not really. Not if she didn't let it. It was merely her overactive imagination.

Yes, she felt isolated at Ravenfell with the caretaker skulking the halls. But she was not going to let that squash her determination to remain.

The village was bustling. The market square hosted a large bubbling fountain. A young girl with pale blonde hair begged her mother for a copper. Her mother relented, handing over the coin. When she did, the girl's eyes lit with joy. She clutched it in her fist, holding it tight as she closed her eyes and whispered something, then tossed the coin in the fountain.

"Do you think my wish will come true, Mama?" the girl asked.

Her mother grinned. "Only if you keep it a secret. Come on. Papa is waiting for us."

She took the girl's hand, and they hurried away, melting within the throngs. Smiling, Victoria stepped up to the fountain and peered into the shimmering water glistening in the morning light. Coins of all shapes and sizes rested on the colorful tile. Every coin represented a wish or hope.

Inspired, she dug into her reticule for a copper. She closed her eyes, the coin between her thumb and forefinger, and whispered a wish she dared not speak aloud. When she opened her eyes, the splash in the fountain was louder than it should have been. Or maybe it only sounded that way because, for a heartbeat, the world had gone still.

A shadow fell across the stone. She hadn't heard anyone approach.

"What did you wish for?"

The voice was low. Male. Familiar. She turned slowly to see Gabriel standing there. Her heart fluttered, startled by his sudden appearance.

Gabriel stood a few feet away, his hands tucked behind his back. His dark coat stood out in the early morning sunshine, the top button was the only one done as though he'd put it on in haste. His shoes—normally polished—were coated in a fine sheen of road dust. The light breeze tousled his hair, making a few strands flutter on the top. And it occurred to her, then, he wore no hat.

She also noticed, for the first time, the cut features of his face. His chiseled jaw clenched tight as he gazed at her with his onyx eyes. His fine-boned cheeks. He was...handsome and yet there was an underlying sense of melancholy about him.

"You startled me," she said, trying to quell her racing heart.

But, she thought, it was not racing merely because he startled her.

"Forgive me. I didn't intend to." His expression remained unreadable, his voice lower. Different. Gentle.

"Did you follow me?"

"Yes." He didn't bother to hide it. "The roads are not always safe. And..." He hesitated. "You seemed troubled this morning. I thought perhaps some company wouldn't be unwelcome."

She blinked. That almost sounded like concern. His reticence in the kitchen flashed through her mind. Though his demeanor had not changed, there was something else there. He looked pale, his features lined with fatigue. As if the walk to the village had taxed him to near exhaustion. Sweat beaded along his forehead and dampened his short sideburns.

"Well, I can manage a short walk and a post without being spirited away," she teased, more lighthearted than she felt.

He didn't return the smile.

She turned toward the post. He fell in step beside her, his hands still firmly tucked behind his back. They crossed the square together. She was acutely aware of his height next to her as well as the sidelong glances they garnered from villagers. He reached the door to the post first, pushing it open. A chime sounded, announcing their arrival. Gabriel stood aside to allow her to enter first. There were no other patrons. Only a young man not much older than her behind the counter sorting packages.

He greeted them with a smile and bright eyes as she approached. "Mornin', miss. Posting a letter?"

"Two, actually," she said. "One to the Crown Hollow Tribune and another to my aunt in the city, if you please."

He accepted them with a nod, glancing between her and Gabriel. "Haven't seen you round here before. Are you new to the area?"

"I've recently come to live at Ravenfell Manor," she said brightly.

The boy's smile faltered. "That crumbling old place?"

Gabriel stiffened beside her.

"Yes," Victoria said. "It belonged to my parents. I hope to restore it."

The boy scratched the back of his neck as he shifted his stance, discomfort creasing his features. "Wouldn't be my choice of places to live."

Her brows drew together. Gabriel remained ramrod straight beside her. "Why is that?"

"Well...you know what they say about it."

"No, I don't," she said, her heart thumping in her chest. "What do they say?"

"Just that it's haunted by the lady who died there. They say her spirit never left." He leaned in a little, voice hushed. "Some folks say she still wanders the west wing, wailing at night for a child lost."

A sharp breath escaped her before she could stop it. A child wailing. A woman wandering the halls. The west wing. Cold chills danced up her spine. She refused to look at Gabriel and instead kept her eyes on the boy behind the counter.

"That's enough," Gabriel said suddenly, his voice like steel.

The boy blinked and stepped back. "Sorry, sir. I meant no offense."

"The lady has business to attend to. She doesn't need to hear ghost stories."

"O'course." He stamped the letters with precision, his features falling. "I'll get this off straightaway."

"See that you do." Gabriel placed a firm hand on her elbow. "Miss Ravenwood?"

She gave a nod of thanks to the young man and allowed Gabriel to guide her outside. The sunlight no longer warmed her quite the same way. They crossed the square in silence, his hand eventually falling away as they passed the fountain. The cheerful voices and clatter of morning business faded into the background, replaced by the echo of that boy's words.

All the effort she'd put into dismissing her fears evaporated like breath on a cold windowpane. She could no longer explain away what the boy had said as simple village gossip. Not after everything she'd seen. Not after the voice in the dark.

A woman, crying for her child. A mirror that shouldn't have been there. A crushed lilac.

She refused to cut a glance to Gabriel. To look at him and confirm her suspicions. Not that he would confirm anything. He kept his emotions in check every moment.

Except when he snapped at the boy. For that one moment, his perfectly polished exterior cracked. And in that crack, she caught something raw. Grief or, perhaps, fear. She couldn't be sure. But she knew one thing.

Gabriel Allward was hiding more than dusty ledgers and silent hallways.

Chapter 11

Gabriel escorted her back to Ravenfell. They didn't speak much as they walked in the late morning sunshine. The words from the young man at the post burned through her still.

When they returned to the manor, she went up to her room. She removed her hat and gloves with practiced ease to keep her hands from shaking. To forget. But it was hard to forget. A sort of nervous energy pulsed through her. As she glanced around her room, seeing the dust and the cobwebs and the worn furniture, she couldn't stay in this room for another minute.

If she sat still too long, she'd go mad. Her mind would wander into places it shouldn't—cold drafts, crying children, ghostly whispers in the dark. She needed something to ground her. Something to keep her occupied while she waited for responses to come in from her advertisement she placed with the Tribune.

But when she went back down the stairs, Gabriel announced lunch was served in the dining room. Since she missed breakfast, her stomach was hollow, and she knew she needed to eat. All through luncheon, the boy's words echoed through her mind. A woman's wail. A child's death. And Gabriel's tone...sharp and icy. A crack in his iron mask for the briefest of moments.

Gabriel served her cold sliced chicken previously prepared with a bit of mustard sauce, sliced fresh fruit, and a pot of tea. The warm scent of the tea was a comfort and a reminder of the home she once had with her parents.

Once he'd served her, he disappeared back into the kitchen, leaving her alone.

When she finished, she decided to spend some time in the garden. If her mother loved it, then perhaps she would as well.

Gabriel returned to clear away the dishes.

"I think I'll dedicate some time to the garden this afternoon," she announced. "Thank you for lunch."

He gave a nod. "The sun is strong today, miss," he said, not quite looking at her. "You'll want a hat."

Victoria paused there a long moment, waiting to see if he'd say anything else. He busied himself with the dishes, turning his back to her as he cleared them away and then headed to the kitchen.

He might not have been wrong about the hat, but she wasn't about to go back upstairs to fetch one. Instead, she headed out the front door and took the same footpath she and her uncle took the day before.

Had it only been that morning when he bid her farewell to return to the city? It seemed as though eons had passed.

She followed the footpath through the vibrant colors of the flowers, enjoying the fragrant smell. Gabriel was right in that it was a hot afternoon and the sun was burning down upon the top of her head.

Surely there was an old garden shed she could rummage through to find a hat.

She continued down the path, past the lilacs that were in full bloom and the bench she and her uncle shared the morning before when he talked of her mother and how she won best in show at the flower festival. Past the hydrangeas with their delicate petals nodding as if in quiet greeting.

As she wandered deeper, the roses sweetened the air. She bent to one bloom, its color a striking pink, and breathed deep. The scent should have soothed her, but there was a stillness in the air that kept her on edge. Then she walked again toward an opening in the bushes. Here, the path opened into a maze of low hedges shaped to perfection. At its heart stood a stone fairy, wings outstretched, mid-flight and forgotten. Beyond the statue half-hidden in overgrowth, a small greenhouse that looked as though it had been neglected for years. Ivy curled over the glass walls, hiding its secrets within.

Perfect, she thought. If there was an old straw hat anywhere, it would be in there.

She headed toward it with purpose, her shoes nearly silent on the cobblestone walkway. At the door, she tried to pull it open.

But the ivy kept it from budging. After a few yanks, she finally got the door open and stepped inside.

Light filtered through the dirt-smudged glass, spilling on the floor in slashes. Forgotten pots were scattered along the work table, still full of dirt. Some with dead plants that had tried to thrive without care and failed. On one end of the bench, gardening tools. A wide spade. A fork.

Something under the bench caught her eye. She bent to get a closer look.

Her breath caught as she picked it up. She turned it over in her hands. The blue dress was faded, the fabric brittle. The face was faded, too. Almost nonexistent. Wasn't there once a smile? A memory tugged at the edges of her mind, but she couldn't grasp it. Her fingers trembled. Why was it here?

The air shifted, dropping to a cold breeze that curled around her. With it came the scent of lilacs, potting soil, a whisper of memory so vivid it stole her breath. A memory of spending the day out here with her mother. Once. Long ago.

Her mother hummed a tune she didn't know, while she sat on the low stool smoothing the doll's hair.

And then a pot crashed to the ground, startling them both. Her mother sucked in a sharp breath and stripped off her garden gloves to investigate the fallen pot on the other end of the greenhouse.

As she did, the girl appeared.

"You said I could play with your doll," the girl said, her voice flat. "You promised."

"I didn't promise." Victoria clutched the doll to her chest, protective.

"You did. You did. You promised!" she wailed, her voice rising unnaturally high as she stomped her foot.

Victoria started to cry.

"Let's go inside, Victoria." Her mother's voice shook. She sounded frightened.

And then her mother hustled her out of the greenhouse.

Victoria held the doll tight in her hands as she glanced around the greenhouse, sensing a presence but not seeing it. The little girl? She'd said her name was Lily.

She heard again the young man's words at the post, sharp and unavoidable.

...wailing at night for a child lost...

"Lily?" The air crystalized when she said the girl's name. She forged onward. "I don't know what happened to you. But I'd like to help you. If I can."

The voice whispered back, *You can't. No one can.*

And then, everything was righted as though nothing at all happened.

That eerie sensation was gone, but it had left a lasting impression on her.

Victoria turned toward the greenhouse door. As she reached for it, a gust of wind blew past. The door slammed shut. She sucked in a breath, dropping the doll, and hurried to it and tried to push it open, but it was stuck. It had taken several tries for her to get the door open in the first place on the outside. Now she was inside and unable to shove it open. Not even an inch.

Trying not to panic, she glanced around the greenhouse looking for something to help her leverage the door. But there was nothing. Only the spade and fork discarded on the bench. On impulse, she snatched the spade, using the tip to wedge in between the door and the frame.

No luck.

Overhead, the sun suddenly disappeared. When she glanced up, she saw there were thick black clouds threatening rain.

Pounding on the door would do no good. There was no one to hear her. Gabriel was still in the house. He hadn't followed her this time. For a moment, she wished he had as her heart drummed in her chest.

Thunder cracked, rattling the glass panes.

She threw her weight against the door to no avail. She tried again, hitting it harder. This time, it was so hard pain lanced through her shoulder. She cried out, holding her arm against her body as she stumbled backward.

Rain pelted the glass ceiling. Soft, at first. Then harder and harder. The roof on the end of the greenhouse leaked, spilling rainwater inside. Lightning sliced across the sky with the sudden thunderstorm followed by the boom of thunder.

She couldn't get out. Clutching her elbows she stepped toward the middle of the greenhouse. Hot tears sprang to her eyes.

Her voice trembled. "Don't panic," she whispered, but there was a rising tightness in her chest that indicated otherwise.

Hopefully, Gabriel would come looking for her. She'd told him she was heading to the garden. But it was likely he wouldn't come after her until it stopped raining. Until then, she was trapped here.

The trees surrounding the greenhouse swayed with the gust of wind. One branch over the roof scraped the glass with a high-pitched screech. With her gaze fixed on it, she stepped back. But the branch was so large, if it came down, it would take most of the roof with it.

She tried the door again. She shouted until her throat was raw.

Another gust of wind.

A loud *crack*.

She looked up just as the branch snapped and came tumbling down. She leapt out of the way. Glass shattered around her as she covered her head. When she took a step toward the bench, her foot slipped and she went down, smacking her head on the cobblestone floor.

The last thing she saw was the faded doll face staring back at her through shards of glass. Then darkness swallowed her whole.

Chapter 12

Gabriel should not have followed her to the village. As the distance expanded between him and the manor, his strength waned, making him weak. His hands shook. His breathing labored. Sweat popped out on his forehead and trickled down his spine. Victoria did not seem to notice. Or if she did, she concealed it.

How could he explain it to her? She wouldn't understand. He could leave the boundary of the manor to visit the village, but only for a short time and never very far.

But he was determined to see her safe, to make sure she made it to and from without incident. And then the young man in the post...telling her the halls of the manor were haunted by the lady who died here.

Well...the boy wasn't wrong. But Gabriel was not ready for that bit of knowledge to come to light.

The sky split without warning. One moment, a frail sun blinked behind gauzy clouds. The next, darkness crashed down as though the heavens had swallowed the light.

Gabriel's first thought was of Victoria. She said she planned to be in the garden. He'd mentioned she wear a hat. But he hadn't seen her after that. He checked her room. Empty. He hurried back down the stairs to the study. Not there.

Perhaps she'd been caught out in the rain on her way back to the manor. Any minute now, she'd come through the door soaked to the bone.

He paced the foyer, the grandfather clock ticking louder with every pass. Thunder cracked. The storm raged. Heart pounding, he stopped, staring at the front door. Willing her to return.

When she still hadn't returned long minutes later, he had to act. He hurried through the kitchen to the back door that exited into the back half of the garden. Rain pelted him as he barreled down the steps. The wind gusted through the garden, stripping petals from their stems like confetti, hurling them into the air in a frenzied dance of ruin.

Panic lanced through him when Victoria was nowhere to be found. By now, his clothes were soaked and his shoes were muddy. But he kept going until he made it to the hedge garden.

He halted there, rain running down his face in rivulets. Then he saw it. The fallen branch through the greenhouse roof.

And his heart lurched.

Certainly, she wasn't in there?

He sprinted toward it calling her name. She didn't answer. The door was wedged shut. He pressed his face against one of the windows, peering through the deluge.

A flash of pale blue against shattered glass. *Oh, saints.*

"Victoria!"

She didn't move. She couldn't hear him.

Adrenaline pumping through him, he went back to the door and grabbed the aging handle. The wind must have slammed it shut. He jerked with all his strength once, twice, three times until finally the door gave and opened. Opening it wide, he secured it with a heavy rock to keep it from blowing closed again.

Inside, his feet crunched on broken glass. How she escaped being slashed to ribbons by the glass, he didn't know. Blood dampened the side of her head.

He scooped her up, cradling her against his chest as he hurried out of the greenhouse and back down the footpath. The rain continued to fall as he made it back to the house. With the heel of his shoe, he kicked the door, slamming it shut.

Rather than carry her upstairs, he headed to the sitting room, the oldest part of the manor, behind the study. There, he gently lowered her down to the settee and pulled off her shoes. Her damp gown clung to her. Her chestnut hair, normally styled to perfection, was plastered against her head, the long lengths dripping down the pillow onto the velvet cushion.

Then he turned to the hearth and quickly got the fire going. It only took a few minutes before the flickering flames warmed the small room.

Gabriel dropped down on his knees, his face inches from hers. Her eyes were closed. Her long lashes curled upward. Reaching for her, he nudged away a damp piece of hair to get a good look at the cut on the side of her head. It didn't look bad, but it would need to be cleaned.

He rose, standing there at her side with his heart racing and his hands clenched. His damp clothes left small circles around him. His soaked shoes left muddy halos on the polished wood.

But she was safe.

He didn't have time to waste. He could already sense her in the shadows, watching. He rushed from the room to find medical supplies. He'd have to hurry before Lenore decided to make an appearance. Once he'd gathered all he needed, plus a plush blanket, he returned to the study, closing the door behind him.

As he dabbed the blood away from her wound, the storm raged on. Though he knew Lenore had nothing to do with the sudden thunderstorm, it was hard not to blame her after the threat.

When he finished, he placed the blanket over Victoria, tucking it around her to keep her warm.

Then he sat on the floor, resting his back against the settee to watch the flames, and wait for her to wake.

Victoria came awake suddenly. Her head throbbed. Her vision swam. She blinked into flickering shadows, uncertain if she'd crossed into some half-lit realm between the living and the lost. She tried to sit up, but her limbs were tangled in a blanket. She flailed, crying out, her thoughts spinning as she grasped for memory.

"Shh."

Gabriel.

Suddenly, he was there. Resting on the narrow edge of the sofa cushion. He grasped her hands in his, holding her steady. A crack of thunder made her jerk. He wrapped her in his arms, holding her tight against him. Against his warmth.

"It's all right."

Her ear was pressed against his chest, listening to the steady rhythm of his heart. First instinct was to shove out of his arms, but he felt so nice. So warm. So safe. Her eyes were drowsy again. Her head still pounding.

Across from her, a warm cheerful fire.

She whimpered again, still trying to right her senses.

His arms tightened around her as he gently rocked her, to comfort her. "You're safe now, Victoria. I'm here."

He said her name.

Something about the way he uttered her name sent a shiver of familiarity through her. As though she'd heard him say her name before.

"Y-you said my name." Her teeth chattered, despite his warmth. She didn't know why.

"I've thought it a thousand times." His voice was quiet in the solitude of the room.

He had?

Her breath pooled in her throat as they clung to each other.

There was something haunting about the way he said her name, the way it lilted off his tongue as though he had not only contemplated it countless times, but said it. With reverence. With a deep-seated need that stirred the dust in the corners of her memory.

A long-forgotten childhood memory surfaced. When she wandered through the misty halls of the west wing, knowing she was not supposed to be there. When she stood in the corridor, holding her favorite doll, staring into the gloom.

Her doll. The gloom. The dark-eyed man who stood still as stone with eyes full of sorrow and despair. Helping her find her way back to her room through the drafty corridors while her parents slept.

He was kind. He was gentle.

He was...Gabriel.

Warmth bloomed in her chest, chasing away the last vestiges of fear. She lifted her gaze to his, searching his unyielding face for signs he was the man in the shadows, the man she had seen lurking in shadows long ago. And she knew he was.

He looked down at her, meeting her gaze. His eyes, usually so guarded, were soft now. Honest.

Lonely.

And that loosed something deep within her. Something she hadn't even known was there. A deep ache pounded through her.

She was lonely, too.

Yet, here they were. Together. Holding on to each other while the storm continued above their heads. Here, in the hush between thunderclaps, they hovered in a fragile peace.

"You've never said it before." Her voice was a cautious whisper, as though saying those words aloud would break whatever spell surrounded them.

"Perhaps I shouldn't have." He looked away toward the fire. The light flickered in the depths of his onyx eyes. "You deserve a better man than me."

His arms dropped away. He shifted to the far end of the settee, leaving her adrift in a sea of emotion.

A thousand questions danced on her tongue, but none of them mattered. Not now.

What mattered was the truth in his voice. The quiet almost-confession in the middle of a storm. The way he had held her like she was precious.

Her hand trembled as she reached for his. He didn't pull away. Their eyes met, but she said nothing as they gazed at each other for a long, intense moment. Gabriel looked away, but he allowed her to hold his hand. He stared at their joined hands as though unsure what to do with the contact. As if the warmth of another person was something he'd long forgotten.

There were walls built around him. Thick, stone walls. She understood. She had them, too. The only sound was the soft crackle of the fire. The relief pounding through her that she was here and not still on the floor of the greenhouse was palpable.

"I'm glad you found me," she murmured.

He slipped his hand away and stood. "You're welcome. I'll bring tea and something to eat. You must be starving."

When he left, she pulled her legs up, wrapping her arms around them. Resting her chin on her knees, she stared into the flickering firelight.

He'd found her. He'd said her name. She knew who he was.

And now, everything had changed.

Chapter 13

The morning brought bright sunshine, as though the previous day's storm had washed away all the torment and shadows. When Victoria rose and dressed that morning, she inspected her head. She had shallow scrapes and nothing more. She was lucky to have gotten out of the greenhouse without serious injury, especially after the tree branch fell.

Her thoughts turned to the night before when she was curled on the settee with the blanket around her while she ate and had tea. Gabriel remained at a distance, his aloof demeanor resuming. When the storm was all but gone, she returned to her room and went to bed.

Yet she couldn't shake the knowledge that he was the figure who had lurked at the edges of her childhood.

Her mother saying with a tremble in her voice, *I don't like this house, Abner.*

Her father's reply, *I thought you loved the gardens, dearest.*

Her retort, *I do but, Abner...something sinister lurks in the shadows.*

And neither of them realizing Gabriel was there all long. The man in the shadows.

He had not aged a day in her twenty-year absence. How was that possible?

She headed to the dining room for breakfast. Gabriel was already there arranging a place setting for her. She wanted to tell him she knew who he was, but the words froze in her throat.

"Good morning, Miss Ravenwood. How do you feel?"

He was back to calling her Miss Ravenwood, which sent a stabbing pain to her heart. As though the progress they'd made the night before was wiped away.

"I'm better, thank you."

He disappeared to the kitchen while she had her tea and scones and remained there, much to her disappointment.

After breakfast, he announced he was going to see about cleaning up the storm damage in the greenhouse. She headed to the study where her father often worked. She closed the door, sealing her inside the silence of the room. She'd spent time here writing her letters to her aunt and the Tribune, but she hadn't *really* looked at the room.

She moved to the window and drew back the thick curtains allowing the morning light to splash inside. Dust motes danced in the sunlight and spilled across the top of the desk. She sat at the desk where she'd left a stack of parchment, an inkwell, and pen where she'd written her letters.

There were drawers on either side. She pulled open the top one where she'd found blank parchment the day before. There was nothing of note so she moved on to the second one. This drawer held old papers—correspondence to her father, letters to her mother, invitations to balls. These were on the desk at one point. She assumed Gabriel stacked them and put them away. Curious, she slid out a letter from the stack. It was addressed to the Honorable Abner Ravenwood.

Dear Sir,

It has come to our attention that your recent inquiries into the restoration of the Parliamentary Committee on Occult Affairs have stirred old fears among those who prefer such things remain forgotten. We urge caution in your continued investigations, especially regarding the Lenore Blackmore incident.

Some doors, once opened, cannot be closed.

Should you require protection for you and your family, you know where to reach us. However, we formally advise you to cease your efforts immediately.

In service to the realm,
Simon de Bauch, Chancellor
Office of Unnatural Matters, Crown Hollow

Her heart rose to her throat as she stared at the letter and read it again and again.

What did it all mean? Who was Lenore Blackmore? And why was her father investigating her?

More questions she was unable to answer. Mysteries she couldn't solve. Uncle Hubert told her that her parents traveled because of her father. Because he was a dignitary.

And the solicitor, Mr. Williams, mentioned the estate was inherited by her father when his father died. And now it passed to her. But did her grandfather know there was something sinister about the estate?

It seemed her father knew there was something going on here since he was searching for answers about Lenore Blackmore.

She replaced the letter and thought about the west wing. Perhaps she would find answers there.

A thorough search of the desk revealed nothing. The locked cabinet gave her pause. She'd have to ask Gabriel for the key to see what was in it.

Or, better yet, see if the key was somewhere in his room.

While he was occupied outside, it was a good time to search his room.

She left behind the study and headed up the stairs, down the long hallway past her room to his at the end. His door was ajar. She hesitated reaching for the knob, but she heard no movement on the other side of the door, so she pushed it open with a creak.

His room was tidy and in perfect order. It was dust and cobweb free. As though this was the only room he gave proper attention. The bed was made, the blankets pulled up and tucked neatly under the pillows, the creases sharp. Across from the bed, the wardrobe. Beyond that, a tall dressing table that looked as though it might have belonged to a woman.

Victoria took a tentative step inside. Heavy draperies covered the window much like in her room. In front of the window, a tufted-back loveseat in a garnet brocade. Next to it, a low round table with a candelabra.

A cursory glance of the bedside table did not produce any type of key. She was hesitant to go through the drawers. That seemed a little too invasive. She took a turn about the room one last time and then started for the door.

As she passed by the bed, something sticking out from under it caught her eye. She paused, peering down at it trying to make sense of what it was. It looked like the corner of a book.

She knelt and reached for it, sliding it out from under the bed.

It was a large book, the same size as the financial ledger, with an aged black leather cover. She recalled that day she found Gabriel in the study how he seemed nervous. Old estate records, he'd called it. He'd hurried past her out of the study with the book.

Victoria stared down at it now, wondering if she dare open it. He said he was relocating them because the mildew was getting to the pages. Why would he store them under his bed?

Unless it was something he didn't want her to see.

Curious, she opened the cover. The first page was blank. Yellowed with age.

As she flipped the page, there was really nothing of note. Lists of things that did, in fact, seem like an inventory. Items for the larder. Supplies for the garden.

Halfway through the book, she stopped cold.

The first entry was written in an old-fashioned hand. The ink faded but still legible.

> *Her cries never stop. The girl's room remains untouched. I cannot bear to close the room and seal it in forever darkness. I failed them both. For that, I remain bound to this place. Forevermore.*

Her mouth went dry. The second entry followed on the next page.

> *The child wandered the west wing again. I tried to remain hidden in the shadows, but she saw me. She wasn't frightened of me. She clutched her doll and looked up at me with bright eyes that reminded me so much of the girl I lost. "Are you the sad man?" she asked. Words were frozen. I nodded. She smiled and something deep inside me cracked. She is like her moth-*

er. Light and bright and full of life. The house watches her now.

The next entry dated days later.

The truth is hidden within the pages. The price was paid for that which could not be undone. Abner knew. He tried to buy more time, but the debt was never repaid.

What price? What truth? She read on. Another entry that looked to be written recently. The ink was not faded.

The house knows her now. It will not let her go. It remembers the Ravenwood blood. It remembers the child who saw the man in the shadows and did not flinch. I wanted to leave—I couldn't leave. And so, I stayed. Waiting. And now, she has returned.

A breath shuddered out of her as she flipped the page. Ice pricked her nape.

Cracks have formed. The veil thins. She is the key, though she does not know it. Spirits awakened. And now...it is too late. If she finds this, it means I've failed to keep her safe.

There were no more entries.

Her breath hung in a pale cloud as she snapped the book closed and pushed it beneath the bed. She stumbled toward the open bedroom door, when the whisper brushed against her ears.

Now you see. Now you know. Nevermore.

Victoria fled.

CHAPTER 14

Her pulse thundered as she sprinted from the room. Her skirts tangled around her legs making her stumble as she barreled through the door, realizing moments after entering the hall she'd left his bedroom door open. If she left it open, he would *know*, he would *see*. She spun back, breath ragged, and pulled it closed.

It was impossible to forget the whisper of words near her ear. The way it clung to her like frost on a brittle morning. Even as she fled, the air felt colder. Heavy. *Aware*.

Her feet carried her down the stairs, her shoe slipping on one of the treads. She stopped herself from falling by gripping the banister and halted there in the middle of the staircase. She pressed a hand against her fluttering heart, willing it to slow as she inhaled, exhaled deep breaths. But it didn't help, and the fear was still there, pulsing through her.

The frigid air, it seemed, chased her down the stairs.

She started again, not knowing where she was going. Only that she had to get out. Down the stairs, into the light. Away from the dark. The shadows. The *death*.

At the bottom of the stairs, she saw the front door open to the early afternoon light. It was raining again. The stoop and beyond glistened with the delicate drops of rain. It dropped off the eaves of the manor house, its rhythmic sound normally smoothing.

Just beyond the door, Gabriel emerged from the garden into the pale afternoon light. His coat was dotted with rain. His hair flattened by the drizzle. In one hand, he carried a jagged piece of broken glass from the greenhouse. In the other, a lantern glowing faintly against the gray afternoon. He looked up as she burst from the door and stumbled into the drizzle. She tripped over her skirt, losing her balance and starting to pitch forward.

"Victoria!"

He dropped the shard of glass and lantern and lunged for her. He caught her, his arms encircling her with startling swiftness. She fell against him, grateful for his warmth, his presence, his everything. She grabbed his coat in her fist, crushing the material in her trembling fingers and pressed her head against his chest, just under his chin. He clutched her, holding her, wrapping his arms around her.

As if he knew what she needed. As if he understood what she'd experienced.

"Something happened," he said. His voice was low, taut, full of tension against her ear. As though seeing her this way—frightened, shaking—unraveled something inside him.

She squeezed her eyes shut, trying to block out the words, the feeling, the terror shifting through her.

"Tell me," he said, more gently this time.

"I...I heard her. She spoke to me."

He stiffened against her. "I think we better go inside."

She shoved out of his embrace and stumbled backward. "No. I don't want to go inside." Her hands fisted at her sides.

He bent to pick up the discarded piece of glass and lantern. "Come inside, Victoria." His voice was low, stern. His expression was guarded.

Gabriel didn't wait for an answer as he headed inside the manor, his feet leaving muddy footprints on the floor and his clothes dripping rainwater in tiny circles. She remained where she was a moment longer, her hands still fisted, as the drizzle coated her from head to toe. Somehow, that didn't matter much.

But if she wanted answers, she had to follow him inside.

Swallowing hard, she stepped back into the manor, closing the door behind her and sealing them inside a deathly silence.

She heard Gabriel rattling around in the kitchen—muffled noises from dishes clanking. Her body was rigid as she started to shiver, the cold seeping into her damp gown. She clutched her elbows, trying to ward off the shivering, but she was chilled to the bone.

Gabriel emerged from the kitchen carrying a tray with a teapot, cups, and scones. He paused there a moment, their eyes meeting. His face was still devoid of emotion.

"Come to the sitting room," he said.

Without waiting for an answer, he headed down the hall, shadows trailing after him. A violent shudder went through her as she forced her feet to follow him.

In the study, he poured tea into the two porcelain cups. He added a lump of sugar to one, stirred, then picked it up and held it out to her. He knew she liked one lump of sugar in her tea. Then he placed a dollop of cream in the second cup and sat on the end of the settee, waiting for her to do the same.

He acted as though this was nothing more than afternoon tea on a bright sunny day. It was not. It was a dark, gloomy day, and she was learning, all too quickly, her newly inherited manor was haunted.

She gripped the cup so tight in her hand, her finger cramped. He sipped, pretending everything was well.

Finally, she blurted, "I read it."

He froze, his gaze on some distant plane she could not see. He refused to look at her as he held his teacup halfway to his mouth, his fingers leeching of color. When he made no response, she forged on.

"The journal under your bed. Your handwriting. *If she finds this, it means I've failed to keep her safe.*" Her voice broke. "What is this place, Gabriel? What *are* you?"

His jaw clenched, the muscles flinching there. Still, he would not look at her.

"Why were you in my room?" His voice was low, accusatory.

She deserved that. "I was looking for the key to the locked cabinet in the study."

"There is nothing there for you to see."

"Then why is it locked, Gabriel?" Still, he did not answer. "You moved that book from the locked cabinet, didn't you? You didn't want me to see it."

"No." His reply was curt, cold.

"Why?" she demanded. Sudden hot tears burned the backs of her eyes. She had almost wanted to trust him and now, this betrayal.

"I hoped you would never find it." His gaze was still fixed on something in the distance. He could not bring himself to look at her.

And that infuriated her. "Because of what it says?"

Silence.

"Gabriel, look at me," she demanded.

Finally, his gaze flickered to hers. In them, she saw a myriad of emotions. Regret. Remorse. Guilt. And something ancient and otherworldly.

"Who are you?" she asked, her voice raspy and soft amid the hush that filled the room.

"You know who I am," he replied.

"But you haven't aged. You hide in the shadows. You vanish when I blink. Are you even alive?"

"I'm no ghost."

"But you're not just a man, either, are you?"

A flicker of something old and sorrowful passed through his eyes. "No."

She remained still, trembling from cold and revelation. "Then what are you?"

He sighed, dragging a hand through his wet hair. "I was bound to this place by a promise I didn't understand. The house...it remembers. It holds on to what it loves and what it fears." He looked past her again, to that place in the room he'd been staring at. "Lenore is both."

Victoria's throat tightened. "And me? What am I to it?"

"You're blood." His voice softened. "The last of the Ravenwoods. You've awakened something that's been dormant for years."

A crack of thunder in the distance made her flinch. "Then why didn't you tell me?"

He put down his cup, rose, and crossed the distance between them in three strides. "Because I wanted to protect you." His hand hovered near her cheek, but didn't touch. "Because I failed once before."

She stared at him, tears threatening once again. "You mean Lenore. Who is she?"

He flinched upon hearing her name.

But there were still questions she had burning through her. Who, exactly, was Lenore? What happened to her? Why was Gabriel trying to protect her—and what from? She pressed her lips together wanting to ask them all, but didn't. She watched his expression intently, as the pain flashed through his eyes for a brief moment before he concealed it.

Finally, he nodded, pain shadowing his features. "She was once like you. Curious. Bright. And the house...it took her."

What did that mean—it took her? How? Why? Fear pierced her, hot and wild.

There was no doubt in her mind something sinister was happening here in this place she thought to call home.

She paused a long moment, then Victoria whispered, "Will it take me, too?"

Gabriel looked at her then—truly looked. In his eyes she saw truth and honesty. "Not if I can help it."

He meant it when he said it. His words were firm, valiant.

A faint muffled whisper wrapped around them. Lenore again? Gabriel's eyes darkened as he continued to look at her.

"Come. Sit with me. Rest. You've had a fright."

Then he turned away and sat once again on the settee. A fright was putting it mildly. She had questions. Numerous questions. He didn't seem to be in the mood to answer them.

But she recognized an olive branch when she saw it. So, she sat near him on the settee. He refilled her cup, warming her tea, and handed it to her. She took it, grateful for the warmth pressing through her hands as she held it close to her face. The steam curled upward, giving her comfort.

They sat in amicable silence for a time, listening to the faint rumble of thunder and the patter of rain outside on the windows.

"The greenhouse will need to be repaired. It is beyond my skill," he said, then, as though that were the most pressing matter.

"Were you able to remove the tree branch?" she asked.

"No. I will need to hire someone to do that as well."

He set aside his teacup, then reached into the folds of his coat and drew something out.

"I found this in the greenhouse."

Her breath caught as he held it out to her. A doll with a faded face, and a faded blue dress. Her doll. She'd left it in the greenhouse.

"I remember this," she whispered. "It was mine. I thought I'd lost it long ago."

She took it reverently and placed it in her lap, cradling it as though it were made of glass.

"When you were a child, I found it in the west wing," Gabriel said softly. "I tried to return it to you, but you and your parents were already gone. Today, it was in the greenhouse."

It did not explain how it ended up in the greenhouse. Perhaps whatever sinister force lurked moved it there.

Something in his voice curled around her, drawing her closer. She thought back to her life here in the manor when she was young.

Though he may not have realized it, Gabriel confirmed the one thing she long suspected—he was part of this house then as he was now.

"Thank you," she murmured, her gaze still fixed on the doll. She could not look up at him.

"The day is late," he said as he got to his feet. "I should prepare dinner."

Before she answered, he left her alone in the room, with nothing more than memory fragments and a relic from her childhood.

CHAPTER 15

The sun came out the following day.

After a long, agonizing night cowering beneath her covers, a hint of light pierced her drawn curtains in her room. Relief trickled through her as she threw off the blankets and rose from the bed. She'd barely slept.

Fatigue pounded through her, but she decided to forge onward. After breakfast, a walk to the local village would be good for her to get some fresh air and stretch her legs. It would also be a good time to check and see if there were any letters for her at the post.

She didn't want to tell Gabriel this, as she wanted time to go alone and to think. To work out everything that had happened to her these last few days in the manor.

When Gabriel was busy in the kitchen, she pulled on her gloves and hat and slipped out the door.

Everything seemed so fresh and bright this morning after the previous day's rains. The lawn still glistened, shining in the morning light. It was a welcome sight after being stuck inside the dark and dreary manor.

Victoria inhaled a deep breath, enjoying the clean breath of air. Her step was a little livelier as she headed down the footpath and into the village.

The village was bustling with morning activity. With the vendors setting up their carts and the people milling about heading to market. But she was interested in the post and headed there first.

The bell jingled her arrival as she headed inside. The same young man was there as the day she posted the letters. He smiled and nodded as she approached the counter. The post office was otherwise empty.

"Good mornin', miss. What can I do for you?" he asked, his eyes were bright and his voice cheerful.

"I came to see if you had any letters for me. Miss Victoria Ravenwood," she said.

"Ah, yes." He nodded and turned away to the wall of mailboxes behind him. He searched through them until he found the one he wanted and pulled it down. "This came just yesterday."

He handed it over. She recognized her aunt's handwriting immediately. Not the sort of letter she was hoping for, exactly.

"Is there nothing else?" she asked.

"'Fraid not, miss. Ain't your gentleman with you today?" His keen gaze glanced around behind her, as if waiting for him to pop into the building unannounced.

"No," she said. "I came alone. I was hoping there were responses to my inquiries to hire staff."

"At the manor?" He drew his brows together.

"Yes. Ravenfell."

"I don't 'spect you'll be getting any responses, miss," he said. "Not with the way things are up there."

Heat pounded through her. "What does that mean?"

"Just that...well...no one seems to keep a job there very long. The hauntings, they say."

Her mouth turned dry as she stared at him. He mentioned the hauntings before when she was posting her letters. "What do you know about the hauntings?"

The boy shrugged. "Not much. Just what I've heard."

"The lady who died there," she said. "What have you heard about her?"

Victoria knew she was prying, but since Gabriel wasn't forthcoming with information, perhaps she could find out something from this young man.

"I think her name was...Loraine? Leena? Something like that. I don't really know much. It was a long time ago."

Lenore. The name whispered through her mind.

"How long ago?" she prodded.

He thought long and hard about it before he answered. He whisked his hand over his smooth chin. "I can't really say. But I know it's been many years."

Clearly, she wasn't getting anywhere with him. "Thank you for your time."

Clutching the letter, she turned toward the door. She almost reached it when he stopped her.

"Oh, miss? I do recall there was another family that lived there long before yours. A man and his wife—they had a little girl, too."

She turned back, pausing to look at him. "Are you sure that wasn't me and my parents twenty years ago?"

"I'm sure. It was before that. Several decades. Maybe more. Reckon the little girl died, too. That's how the story goes, anyhow. I heard tell the man was so distraught after his lady wife died, he never left the place again. Don't know what ever happened to him."

Victoria thought she knew.

A shiver of ice moved through her as though someone had walked over her grave.

She took her time walking back to the manor. With every step, the dread increased. A shiver ran through her at the thought of returning to that desolate place where shadows crept and mist whispered along the halls. She had longed for Ravenfell. Now it felt like it was swallowing her whole.

Her aunt's letter was clutched in her hand. She glanced down at it, saw it was wrinkled from her tight grip. What news did her aunt have for her?

For the briefest moment, a flash of longing went through her. Of the sun-splashed parlor in their brownstone in the city. The hum of the noise from the streets. The soft warm glow of the lamplight in her room.

If she wrote to her uncle telling him she'd changed her mind about Ravenfell, she had no doubt he would welcome her back with open arms. Her aunt would be more than delighted to find her a husband.

But that's not what she wanted at all. Living her life under false pretenses was something she could never accept. The idea of a husband being found for her filled her with defiance. She preferred not to live in the shadow of her larger-than-life aunt.

Victoria sighed. Even as she dreaded the manor, she could not stop her feet from carrying her toward it. Toward an uncertain future in a place that was likely haunted.

When she arrived back home, she headed to the parlor to sit and read the letter her aunt sent her. She lowered herself to the chair, ripped the letter open, and began to read. It was nothing more than her aunt's ramblings about city life, her uncle returning to his banking job, the dinner party she threw for several of his colleagues and a few more in high society.

I was so pleased to meet the Honorable Earl of Berkhampstead. Perhaps you've heard of him? He remembered your father. It seems they traveled abroad together attending galas and the like. He was quite interested in you when I mentioned you'd inherited Ravenfell and asked if you would mind ever so much if he called on you. Of course, I told him yes, that you certainly wouldn't mind—

Victoria stopped reading as a strangled gasp escaped her. Oh, Gods, what had she done? And why was she telling strangers—an earl, no less!—about her and Ravenfell Manor? She crumpled the letter in her fist out of frustration.

How could Aunt Eloise do this to her? Now, Victoria would be on edge wondering if and when this earl would make an appearance. She didn't need him here snooping around, nor did she want that sort of intrusion here. If he did show up, she'd then have to explain his arrival to Gabriel.

He'd warned her once before the house didn't like changes or accept them very well. How would this earl's arrival affect the manor? Would the ghostly presence of Lenore ramp up, then?

She didn't know. She shot to her feet and paced the small area of the parlor, nerves jangling.

"Is everything all right?"

Gabriel's voice from the doorway startled her. She yelped, pressing a hand against her racing heart as she halted.

"Oh! You scared me." She blew out a breath. He was very good at skulking about the manor, unheard.

"Apologies, miss. I didn't mean to. You seem agitated. Everything all right?" he asked again.

"I've received a letter from my aunt."

He lifted a dark brow and, for a moment, amusement flickered over his face. "Judging by your face, I take it the news was less than delightful."

She wanted to laugh, but somehow kept it from bubbling up her throat. He didn't know just *how* distressing the letter was. And she couldn't bring herself to tell him. She couldn't share with him their solitude might be invaded by the Earl of Berkhampstead. So, she played it off with a smile.

"My aunt is…well, she doesn't think I should be living here."

Curiosity flickered across his face. "And why is that?"

"I'm a single woman. I'm sure you can guess why."

"Ah, of course. She thinks you should be married."

"Married and living in the city, bearing children like a proper wife." The words tumbled out of her, unbidden. She hadn't realized how bitter she felt about that until she said it aloud. "I'm sorry. I shouldn't have said that."

He leaned against the doorframe, folding his arms across his chest giving him a causal air that seemed quite out of character. Perhaps things had shifted between them, allowing him to feel a bit more comfortable around her.

"Don't be. I'm sure it puts you in a difficult situation having her wanting to marry you off."

He sounded as though he understood her plight and empathized with it.

"Yes, it does."

His dark eyes remained on hers, studying her intently. "Do you not wish to marry?"

It was an unexpected question. He sounded wholly curious and interested in her answer. Though why, she did not know. As she considered her answer, she fiddled with the crumpled paper in her hand. Did she wish to marry? It seemed like an unobtainable goal. Something she had never really considered. After the tragic death of her parents, her life came to a halt.

"I think..." she started, choosing her words carefully. "I think perhaps someday. If—" She stopped herself from saying *if the suitor is the right man.*

Her gaze met his. Was he the right suitor? She wasn't sure. But she relished how he caught her in the doorway and held her in his arms. She recalled, with a sudden, sharp memory, there was something otherworldly in his scent, like frost caught in sunlight. Crisp, fleeting, and gone before she could name it. It gave her comfort, soothed her, made her want to keep him close.

And yet, she needed to keep him at a distance.

"If?" he repeated, his voice low.

She smiled then, pushing away the thoughts. "It's nothing. I'm just being silly."

"I doubt that." He pushed off the doorway then. "I have work to do in the greenhouse this afternoon."

It was an announcement he intended to be outside most of the day. She nodded as he walked away.

As Gabriel disappeared down the hall, her gaze drifted upward toward the west wing. Perhaps it was time to stop being afraid of shadows and walk straight into them.

CHAPTER 16

When she knew Gabriel was outside the manor and deep into the garden at the greenhouse, Victoria left the parlor and headed up the stairs. Her nerves jangled with every step as she ascended, her hand on the banister and her eyes lifted toward the west wing.

She did not know what she would find.

She turned right and paused at the entrance of the long hallway that led through the west wing of the sprawling manor house. Her eyes landed on the closed door of the child's room.

A shudder went through her.

She would not open that door today.

As she headed down the shadowy corridor, fog lifted from the creaking floorboards, swirling around her ankles as though it were the most natural thing. Her heart rose to her throat, but she was determined to keep her wits about her.

A sudden cold settled in the air. Her breath turned to smoke. She halted, just past the girl's bedroom. Her hand clenched into fists as her heart picked up speed.

"I know you're here," she whispered, her breath crystalizing in the air. Then, almost as an after thought, she added, "Lenore."

It was hard to describe, but there seemed to be a...presence surrounding her then. The shadows deepened in the corridor. Fog lifted in spiraling tendrils from the floor. The only sound was the creak of the old floorboard under her step, and then—too softly for certainty—the breath of someone who wasn't there.

"Whatever's happened to you—whatever the reason—I want to know. I want to help."

A low laugh. Almost as though it were a cackle.

Dear sweet child. You cannot help me.

The voice was quiet, mellifluous. Victoria was certain she had heard it before. It stirred something buried—half-memory, half-nightmare—from long ago, when she was small and the manor whispered lullabies to no one.

She forged on, her steps solid and sure across the wooden floor. She paused at the middle room, her hand on the cold knob. She inhaled a deep breath, expelled it, then wrenched the knob and eased the door inward.

It creaked, the old hinges groaning with the effort. The door opened to a darkened room. The interior hosted nothing more than shapes of furniture. She wished she'd thought to bring a candle with her to light her way. But to retreat now would be to surrender—to fear, to shadows, to the house itself.

Victoria stepped into the threshold of the room, her eyes glancing around it as she tried to make out the shapes. A window on the far wall covered in thick drapes that were shut against the light. A four-poster bed on one wall, stripped bare. A wardrobe across from it, the doors shut tight. As her heart continued to throb, she moved deeper into the room and stepped to the wardrobe. She pulled open the door.

Nothing.

Closing it with a snap, she turned away and examined the rest of the room. The wallpaper was old, peeling. It had seen better days. But from the low light, she was able to make out a faded floral design. As though this room had belonged to a woman. Or perhaps it was a guest room.

Back in the hall, she pulled the door closed and continued her exploration.

The next door was at the end of the hall, situated away from the other two doors. As though it were a large suite. Perhaps it was.

Cold permeated the air. Something brushed against her as it flitted past.

Lenore?

She wasn't sure.

Her hand landed on the knob. She twisted and pushed open the door. It thumped against the wall.

The room was a yawning dark chasm. Uninviting. And yet, she was unable to stop herself from stepping inside. She paused there, her gaze scanning the contents of the room.

It was, in fact, a large two-room suite. This was meant for the lord and lady of the manor alone.

She was faced with the sitting room first. Velvet curtains blocked out the light from the double window. She drew back the velvet drapes, fingers trembling slightly, and revealed panes of glass smudged with age and sorrow.

But when she opened the curtains, afternoon light flooded the room, brightening it. The view was that of the back garden. Vibrant colored blossoms swayed in the breeze.

Victoria turned back, her gaze sweeping over the room. The walls were papered in a muted damask, faded slightly from time. The air was musty from the room being closed up for years, ignored. Forgotten. The threadbare rug underfoot once had a vibrant pattern. It, too, was faded from time and neglect.

A pair of tufted armchairs, the upholstery worn but loved, were angled toward the marble fireplace, now cold and dark, though she still got a hint of ash and lilacs lingering there in the hearth. Between the chairs rested a low table bearing a silver tea service dulled by age and non-use. A forgotten book rested next to it. As if the reader placed it down with the intention of returning to read with a cup of fresh tea.

A walnut writing desk was on the other side. The surface was spotless save for a stack of yellowing papers, neatly organized. A quill and inkwell were next to the papers. Ready and waiting for the occupant of the room to return and reply to all the remaining correspondence. Shelves were full of leather-bound books, trinkets, and a small clock that continued to tick away the hours in the heavy quiet of the room.

Everything seemed to muffle out the noise of the outside world.

Even as she stood examining the space, her breath continued to turn white.

And that presence that seemed to follow her everywhere was there. Watching. Waiting.

There were no personal effects here, either. No portraits on the walls or the bookshelves. Nothing on the desk to indicate the occupant.

She moved deeper into the area, heading for the bedroom where the double bed dominated the center.

The first thing that caught her eye was the oil painting of a young woman with a vibrant expression. Her dark locks curled around her head and spilled over her shoulders, a smile curling her pale lips. Her eyes, the color of ink, peered out from the portrait. Her gown was cerulean, trimmed in lace at the cuffs that stopped at the elbow. Whoever she gazed at while she sat for the portrait made her happy. That much was obvious.

"Lenore?" Victoria asked, her voice quiet in the hush.

It was impossible not to sense the phantom that followed her, watching to see what she would do next. Victoria, though, remained where she was as she took in the expansive space.

It was a grand, timeless sanctuary. The high ceilings were crowned with intricate molding. The massive four-poster bed dominated the space, its dark mahogany frame carved with ivy and rose motifs. Heavy garnet velvet drapes cascaded from the canopy.

On one side, a lady's vanity that was dusty from neglect. Crystal perfume bottles lined it like perfect soldiers in a row. Most of the contents had evaporated. Next to the bottles, a silver hairbrush. All of it resting on a lace runner. Nearby, a chaise lounge in pale pink damask that looked like it was inviting once. Ready for the lady of the room to rest and put up her feet after a long day.

Twin wardrobes flanked the inner wall. One for silks and petticoats. The other for cravats and waistcoats.

And still, Victoria's breath turned to smoke before her.

And still, the spectral phantom hovered nearby.

But she was not afraid of it. Of *her*. For Victoria was certain the apparition following her was Lenore.

Turning, she saw the lord's writing desk beneath a series of portraits. Victoria moved closer, a sudden sense of familiarity clanged through her. She stared up at the one in the center. The one with the familiar face, the eyes, the thick dark hair. He wore an out-of-fashion red waistcoat and a perfect, crisp white cravat. His expression was stern, aloof. He stood stiff, one hand at his side. The other bent in front of him.

But as Victoria looked into the eyes of the portrait, she knew instantly who he was.

Her stomach twisted. The room spun slightly.

How long had he been here? How long had he been watching, waiting, guarding?

The walls shivered, as if the house breathed in response to her knowing. She stepped back, heart hammering, the truth clawing up her throat.

The man in the portrait was Gabriel.

And he had never aged.

CHAPTER 17

S he dashed from the room, the cold draft following on her heels. Once she was back in the hall, she closed the door with a snap and leaned against it, the fear pounding through her. Her hands shook as a chill raced through her. She knew Lenore was there. Hovering. Waiting. Watching. Knowing.

"Please," she whispered, though she wasn't sure what she was asking for.

He lied to you, didn't he?

Her voice, sharp and dark, whispered near her ear. Then the lilting laugh echoed through the hall on a disappearing note.

Victoria clutched her elbows, a shudder pulsing through her.

Her feet pounded the ancient, creaking floor as she made her way out of the west wing and back into the main part of the manor. A breath of relief escaped her as she sagged against the wall.

Sunlight slanted there, fractured by the dirty windows in the hall. It should have felt like peace, but it didn't.

She thought back to her first day here, when she insisted on a tour. Gabriel knew his portrait hung in that room. That's why he didn't want her to start there. To see. To know. He must have been so relieved when she didn't make it past the child's room.

The sinister feeling she got in that room was enough to make her never want to return.

And yet, her curiosity was more than she could bear. She had to know what else lay within those rooms.

Now she knew for certain Gabriel was the sorrowful figure who had lingered in the shadows of her childhood. What she didn't understand was how her parents never saw him.

That wasn't entirely true. Her mother sensed something about this house. She feared staying and urged her father to leave Ravenfell behind, perhaps even sell it. Her father, being pragmatic, agreed with his wife and left. The manor was his inheritance from his father, and so, he was unable to sell it. He hung on to it for years waiting to pass it down to her.

Victoria was starting to put the pieces of her childhood memories back together as she remembered more and more. Lenore was bound to this house. So was Gabriel. What she did not know was how they were connected.

The boy at the post mentioned a husband and his wife who died. A man who never left the manor after her death. And there was a child. A child who also died?

She didn't know.

"Victoria?"

Gabriel's voice jarred her out of her thoughts. She came back to her senses and glanced down the length of the stairs to see him standing at the foot gazing up at her with his dark, soulful eyes.

"You look pale. Are you well?" he asked.

She pressed a cold hand against her cheek. Her fingers still trembled. She wasn't ready to confront him about the portrait. "I'm fine. Just a bit tired."

The lie was a kindness.

"Perhaps rest is in order after luncheon," he suggested. "It's ready in the dining room."

It was a welcome distraction. She dropped her hand and started down the stairs, taking the steps slow and one at a time. Her mind drifted back to the portrait and the way he looked in it.

She missed a step, her heel sliding off the edge. She started to fall, gripping the handrail tight to halt her tumble. Suddenly, he was there as he bounded up the stairs. His arms wrapped around her to steady her, making her fall against his chest.

A strangled gasp gurgled up her throat. Either from the near fall or the fact he was holding her against him. She clutched his sleeve, her heart tumbling at both his nearness and her misstep.

She was uncertain how he managed to move so fast, but she was grateful. She tilted her head up. Their faces were inches apart.

"Careful. These old stairs are treacherous."

"Thank you," she managed, her voice but a whisper.

But that's not what she wanted to say. She wanted to tell him she saw his portrait and that he was exactly the same as he was now. And *hers*. She wanted to tell him knew Lenore haunted these halls.

But she didn't. She remained silent as he took her hand and walked with her down the remaining steps. At the foot, he released her.

He made a motion toward the dining room. "Ready for luncheon?"

She nodded and followed him. As she did, she felt the ghostly presence of Lenore behind her.

That night, a storm came. Soft, at first, with faint rumbles of thunder. Lightning lit up her window, casting an eerie flashing glow across her bedroom floor. Unable to sleep, she shoved the blankets down and rested on the bed's edge.

Her room was cold.

She recognized that cold.

Rising, she snatched her dressing gown off the end of the bed and pulled it on. She put on her slippers and grabbed the single candelabra on her bedside table. The flame flickered as she whisked open the door and peered into the dark hall.

The manor was quiet.

As she stood in the threshold, she glanced down the length of the hall to Gabriel's room. Light slashed into the hall. His door was open. She headed to it and peered inside. But it was empty. He wasn't there.

Her footsteps were light as she made her way to the stairs. Holding the candle in one hand, she gripped the handrail in the other, taking care to make slow, methodical steps until she reached the bottom.

Pausing, she glanced toward the darkened parlor. She heard faint notes of the piano. As though someone tapped the keys. Not a tune. Just a note here and there.

"I'm not afraid of you." But even as she said it, the fear clotted the back of her throat.

She turned away from the parlor and headed for the sitting room. The thought of the comfortable old sofa and a warming fire sounded good. Like the best way to wait out the storm.

As she rounded the corner, she saw faint light flickering from the doorway. As though a fire was already lit in the hearth.

Gabriel?

If he was there, she wasn't certain she wanted to disturb him. But then, having him for company would help ease her restless mind.

When she entered the room, she halted. There he was, on the sofa, a tattered volume in his hand and the firelight illuminating his features. When she entered, he looked up. Surprise flickered through his gaze as he put down the book and rose.

"Did the storm wake you, miss?"

He'd called her Victoria earlier that day. She preferred he use her given name than call her miss. But she didn't correct him.

"I've been awake for some time. I'm sorry to disturb you. I should return to my room," she said.

"No, please." His urgent voice stopped her from leaving. He motioned to the seat next to him. "Sit with me. We can pass the time together listening to the storm."

She placed her candelabra on the low table next to the settee and then lowered onto it on the opposite side of him, drawing her legs up underneath her. He picked up his book again, his gaze focused on the pages in the low lamplight of the room.

"What are you reading?" she asked, unable to stand the silence.

"A book of poetry. It's called *Celestial Hymns.*" He handed the open book to her.

She took it and scanned down the page. It seemed to be poetic tales of celestial beings written in fragmented verse. One of a girl born of starlight and moonlight. *Born of blood under a ruined sky.* A lyrical, lovely piece of poetry. She handed him back the book.

"Where did you find it?"

"In the study."

She recalled the expanse of bookshelves but hadn't examined them that close when she was searching the desk.

"I can't recall the last time I read a book," she mused.

"Pity that."

She glanced at him to see a smile tugging at the corner of his mouth. It was the first time she'd seen him actually smile.

"I love a good tale," he said.

"Oh?" She was intrigued. "What's your favorite?"

"Tales of high adventure," he said.

"And perhaps swashbuckling pirates?" she teased.

"Perhaps," he said. "I rather liked *The Corsair.*"

She tilted her head. "By Lord Byron?"

He nodded once.

She recognized the title, though she had never read it. A tale of adventure and revenge. Romantic and dark. But as she considered the name and its author, a small knot formed in her chest. *Hadn't that been published over a century ago?*

He went on, describing other books he'd read. Tales she vaguely remembered from dusty schoolroom lists or antique bookshops. All of them, evidently, housed within the manor's walls.

If he had truly been here for years—decades, even—then perhaps reading was his only escape. A portal to other lives, other places. A distraction from the oppressive quiet of Ravenfell's long-forgotten halls.

She leaned back, letting his voice wrap around her like warmth against the cold storm beyond the window. He spoke with reverence, with the quiet delight of someone who had few joys left. There was something beautiful, and unbearably sad, about the way his eyes lit when he mentioned a favorite tale.

And yet, with every word, that knot in her chest pulled tighter.

As the storm pounded the roof and lightning flashed in the windows, she forgot about haunted passageways and aged portraits and the cackle of a disembodied voice. There was only the two of them, and she found she quite liked this part of him that adored fine literature.

A clap of thunder startled her, making her head snap up.

"Just thunder," he murmured. "Sounds like the storm is almost over."

Indeed, it sounded as though the rain slowed. A distant clap of thunder. A faint flash of lightning. And then she stifled a yawn. And though she was tired, she refused to leave his side. Being in his presence calmed her, comforted her, made her want to stay by his side. As she listened to him talk—he had never said so many words—she sensed they'd made a connection. Their relationship had taken a bit of a turn.

She liked it.

She liked him.

"I've bored you with my fictional tales," he said when he saw her try to hide her yawn.

"Not at all." Her eyes were heavy, the fatigue pressing through her.

"I've prattled on long enough, I should think. Tell me something of yourself."

"Me?" The word squeaked out of her.

"Yes, you." He paused then, contemplation crossing his face. "What happened to your parents?"

The question surprised her, making her wince.

"I'm sorry. I didn't mean to upset you—" he started.

"It's all right," she said, hastily. "It's just that I hadn't spoken of it to anyone."

"You don't have to now."

"But I want to. I need to." She drew her knees up, encircled them with her arms and rested her chin there. "They had been traveling. My father was on some sort of diplomatic trip. I never quite could keep up with their social calendar. They'd returned late that night."

She paused, swallowing hard, as though she could still smell the acrid tang of smoke deep in her nose.

"I'm not sure how the fire started. But the old butler...he pounded on my bedroom door. It was the middle of the night, you see. When he..." She paused here, as her breath hitched.

He moved closer to her to give her courage and strength.

"When he opened the door, the heat was unbearable. Smoke poured inside my room. If it hadn't been for Reginald..." Her words trailed off as she swallowed the sob that wanted to erupt.

"They didn't make it out?" he guessed.

She shook her head. "No. The house burned to the ground. We—I—lost everything."

She hadn't expected the hot tears to burn the backs of her eyes, but there they were. She took a deep breath, expelled it.

"I'm so sorry," he said, his voice soft in the quiet of the room. He moved to reach for her, then drew his hand back, placing it in his lap. The firelight danced on his face full of empathy. And maybe a little pity.

"If it hadn't been for my aunt and uncle, I'm not sure where I would have gone. They took me in." She huffed out a humorless laugh. "And now, here I am. An orphaned heiress."

"I'm glad you're here," he said, and then pressed his lips together as if he was surprised by his sudden admission.

"You are?"

"Certainly. Now I have someone to enjoy my cooking again." He gave her a weak smile.

She did laugh that time, surprised at his jest.

Now that storm had passed, calm descended on the manor once again. She stifled a yawn.

"Well, I should head upstairs."

She rose, heading for the door, but his voice stopped her.

"Victoria?"

She turned back. Their eyes met over the short distance. For the briefest of moments, she thought she saw adoration glinting in his gaze. He started to say something, then pressed his lips together.

Finally, he said, "Sleep well."

"Goodnight, Gabriel."

It seemed perfectly normal to be on a first name basis with him.

As she walked through the doorway, she was acutely aware of the sudden icy air. She shuddered. A creak overhead, which seemed odd. She glanced up and saw the old chandelier in the foyer swinging slightly.

Behind her, she heard Gabriel's book hit the floor and his hurried footsteps as though he sensed something was about to happen.

Before she took another step, the chain holding the chandelier snapped with a loud crack, the wood around the bolt splintering. As she drew in a sharp breath, Gabriel's arms were around her, pulling her out of the way just as the chandelier crashed against the floor and shattered.

A scream ripped from her throat as she turned into him. He wrapped his arms around her, holding her shivering form against him. She buried her face into his chest.

"It's all right," he said into her hair. "I've got you."

His voice, low and steady, wrapped around her. She clung to him. Not just out of fear from the near-miss, but something else. Something unspoken. Something deeper.

Affection. The beginnings of affection tugged at heart.

"What...what is happening?" she breathed.

She tilted her head up, their eyes colliding. In his gaze she saw it. Longing. Regret. Loneliness. A tenderness he didn't try to hide that split her heart in two. In that instant, she understood. He felt the same.

Without thinking, she lifted on tiptoe, drawn by that longing and tenderness buried deep in his eyes. Her lips parted, her breath catching as she reached for him.

He pulled away, sharp and sudden, as though it pained him. "No, Victoria."

The words were barely above a whisper, but they cleaved through the air like a blade. He turned from her, his back rigid, his shoulders trembling ever so slightly.

It wasn't rejection. It was something else. Something carved from guilt and centuries of solitude.

She stood there, suspended between desire and confusion, her heart hammering like a trapped bird. Something inside her said *he wants this, too*, but he believed he couldn't have it.

"I'm sorry. I—"

He spun toward her, his eyes blazing brightly. "No. Forgive me. It's not you. It's...you don't understand what I am."

A breath shuddered through her lips, the image of the portrait flaring bright in her mind. "I *do* understand. I know who you are. You don't frighten me. You didn't then. You don't now."

He raked a shaking hand down his face, then turned away. Silence pressed around them. She remained rooted in place, her hands at her sides as the temperature shifted again. As though Lenore circled her.

"You don't understand—" he started.

"You're not just the caretaker," she said, her breath pluming. "You're something more. Something…else."

She doesn't deserve to know.

The words echoed around them. He spun back toward her, shadows pooling in his eyes.

"It's this house. Once it snares you, it doesn't let go. Victoria—" He stepped toward her, to close the distance, but the house groaned in response.

"It hasn't let go of you?" Her voice shook in the shadowy darkness.

"No. It hasn't. It won't."

He sounded so sad, so desolate it sent a pang right to her heart. Her throat tightened.

"Tell me. I want to know."

Gabriel raked his fingers through his hair, making the ends stick up. "A ghost. But not the kind that fades."

Not the kind that fades. The words echoed like a curse. A shadow trapped in flesh. A man on borrowed time.

That laugh followed. Maniacal. As though it—*she*—understood who and what he was.

"Go to bed, Victoria. I'll clean this up." His voice was terse, hard. Not at all like the man who spoke to her of fantasy worlds and swashbuckling pirates.

Terror lodged tight in her chest as she fled up the stairs. Behind her, the wreckage of the broken chandelier remained a shattered reminder something unseen watched, waited, and would not be ignored.

And below, Gabriel stood alone in the shadows, the firelight flickering across his face, illuminating the ache he could no longer hide.

CHAPTER 18

Victoria skipped breakfast. She knew Gabriel was waiting for her to make an appearance in the dining room, but she couldn't face him. Not after last night.

She was a coward.

Instead, she put on one of her favorite day dresses and tied on a bonnet and headed out the front door to the gardens. She needed fresh air and fresh perspective. She needed to get the enigmatic Gabriel out of her mind. And she needed to pretend, for one moment, there was not a strange presence haunting her home.

Regret pounded through her most of the night. How could she be so foolish to think he wanted to kiss her? She replayed it over and over in her mind. The way he held her, whispered in her hair. The way he looked at her with raw, unabashed longing. She was certain he felt the same as her. That he longed to kiss her as much as she wanted to kiss him.

But, no. She couldn't want that. *He* didn't want that.

There was something sinister going on here and she refused to become ensnared in it.

Even though she was likely already ensnared in it. Whatever *it* was.

In the foyer, she noticed Gabriel had removed the broken chandelier. The only remnants of it was the scuffed floor where it landed.

With the sun shining brightly in the brilliant blue sky, she headed down the footpath to the garden. Everything was still damp from last night's storm. The flowers were blooming in vibrant colors, emitting their sweet fragrance.

It gave her pleasure to know her mother planted most of this garden and tended it herself. She smiled at the thought as she moved down the path.

To her left, the bushes rustled. She halted there, peering at the greenery waving in the faint breeze. Overhead, a raven cawed as it flapped through the sky, its dark feathers gleaming in the morning light. She watched it fly overhead, then she saw the path. Overgrown. As though it had been forgotten.

Instantly, that sense of something not being right rose within her, burning in the center of her chest.

You want to know the truth, don't you?

Lenore. Her voice floated through the gardens as though she followed her out here.

Taunting her.

Her mouth went dry as she stared at the bushes covering the gravel path. It was different from the one she stood on. Not well-maintained like the rest of the garden.

Yes, she wanted to know the truth. Hadn't she been hunting for it since all the strange happenings began?

Victoria stole a glance over her shoulder at the colorful foliage around her. Gabriel was nowhere in sight. Perhaps he was still rattling around in the kitchen. Good. That would give her time to explore. To find out exactly what was down that ominous gravel path.

She pushed aside the branches, their damp leaves leaving wet droplets on her sleeves. It was so overgrown, she had to fight her way down the path, but she felt certain it was leading her somewhere. To something important.

The raven followed above her.

Ahead, the oak tree stretched into the sky, its branches reaching outward providing significant shade from the harsh afternoon sun, as this side of the garden was on the west. The closer she got, the more her heart pounded.

The raven moved ahead of her, perching in a low branch and cawing as if to announce her arrival.

Then she saw it. The two-foot iron fence that had seen better days sectioning off what appeared to be a forgotten cemetery.

She froze there, staring at the two headstones. The engraved lettering was faded. She could not make it out from where she stood. Swallowing hard, she forced her feet to move. A gate hung by one hinge, as though a violent storm had ripped it apart. She pulled it open and stepped inside the small area.

The raven watched. Waited. Its keen eyes fixed on her.

The grass was still wet, but she didn't care as she dropped to her knees. Moss covered the engraving, hiding the words. She reached out and brushed it away, then read the engraving on the first headstone.

Lenore Blackmore Allward, Beloved wife

And the second, smaller marker.

Lily Everleigh Allward, Our brightest light

The girl had been eight years old. Both headstones marked their passing over a hundred years ago. Her breath hitched as she pressed cold fingertips to her lips. A wife. A child. Gone in the same year.

And as she read the surname, Allward, once again, her blood ran cold. She stood, unsteady, her skirt damp. Was this why the house clung to him? Why he had not aged? Why he mourned as though their deaths were yesterday?

And now she was part of it. Bound by knowledge, by memory, by the manor's will.

Overhead, the raven squawked and flapped away. A portent.

Behind her, wind stirred the branches. The scent of lilacs wafted by. A whisper on the air.

Now you know.

Victoria ran back the way she'd come, the branches flapping against her as she shoved them out of the way. One smacked her in the face, scratching her cheek. She'd had enough. Enough of this house. This mystery. This *haunting*. Her gut clenched with acid dread as she ran, hot tears burning her eyes.

The front door banged closed behind her and for a breath, she worried Gabriel would hear and follow her. But she didn't stop as she headed to the study where she closed the door behind her with a snap.

She needed to be alone. She needed to find a way out.

At the desk, she dipped the quill into the ink and started to scrawl the letter in her shaking hand. A letter to her uncle. To tell him she'd made a mistake coming here, hoping for independence. A life of her own. Bitterness rose in her throat. Wouldn't her aunt feel victorious at her failure.

When she finished writing the letter, telling him she would be making her way back, she folded it, sealed it with wax and stood. She slid it into her pocket.

When she pulled open the door, Gabriel stood on the other side, his hand ready to knock. She emitted a yelp of surprise.

His eyes were wide, full of concern, as he looked over her disheveled appearance. Then his brows drew together.

"What's wrong?" he asked.

"Nothing." She shoved passed him and stumbled into the hallway, her feet thumping on the floor. "I'm going out."

To the post. To send off her letter. To see the young worker there once again. Perhaps he would ground her in reality, for she was not living in reality in this house. She was living a nightmare.

Gabriel followed. "Victoria, wait—"

"No," she snapped, not turning. "I will not wait. I'm going."

"Where?" His voice shook, as though he was terrified of her leaving.

Let him be. She flung open the front door and turned to face him one last time. "To post a letter. And then I'm returning to the city, where I belong."

The moment she delivered the news, the front door slammed shut so hard, it rattled the frame. Victoria gasped and stepped back, her heart suddenly in her throat. She reached for the knob, but it wouldn't open. As though the door was stuck.

Tears blinded her. "Let me out!"

Never.

Lenore's frigid presence surrounded her. Determined, she pulled on the door again. Still, it would not budge.

"Please, let me out." A sob hitched through her.

You can never leave. You are bound here. Just as he is.

In the parlor, the piano played a mournful tune. The notes rising to a crescendo. Finally, she crumpled to the floor, her head in her hands as she sobbed.

"Lenore, enough!" His sharp tone cut through the music.

It stopped abruptly.

He crouched next to her, sitting on the floor and wrapping an arm around her shoulders. They sat like that for a long moment as she cried into her hands. Though she didn't want him near her, she admitted his presence soothed and calmed her. He waited, silent, until she finally lifted her head, brushing away the tears in a fit of fury.

She preferred he not see her like that.

"She died here, didn't she?" Victoria asked. She braved a glance at him.

He sat still as a statue, his arm still draped around her shoulders. His stony expression revealed nothing.

"Lenore was your wife," she continued. "And you had a daughter. Lily."

Pain creased his features, as though hearing this drove a blade straight through him. He dropped his arm and shot to his feet, his back to her. Rigid. Taut. Gabriel pushed a hand through his hair, leaving it in disarray. He refused to face her. He didn't want to hear the girl's name from her lips.

"Yes." The word came out in a hiss of a whisper.

"What happened to them?" she asked.

"Please don't ask me to explain." His voice was terse with a hint of anger. "I cannot."

"Why?" she demanded, tired of the half-truths. She got to her feet, her hands fisted at her sides. "Why are you still here when they are not?"

He spun to face her, fury creasing his normally passive features. "Do not ask that of me. *Ever*."

Then he was stalking away, up the stairs. She watched his disappearing form as he turned into the west wing. Moments later, a door opened and slammed.

She turned back to the front door and tried the knob. It opened with ease. She stepped once again into the morning light.

Chapter 19

At the post, she intended to send the letter in her pocket. She intended to get her life back. But when she entered, and the bright-eyed young man behind the counter greeted her, she lost her nerve.

"Nice to see you again, Miss Ravenwood. I have a few letters for you."

When he handed them to her, she saw one was from her aunt. Her gut clenched. The others were responses to her advertisement in the Tribune.

"Anything else I can do for you?" he added.

She plastered on a smile. "No, thank you. Just a mail pickup."

When she turned to go, he said, "I hope things are well for you, miss."

Things were certainly not well for her. But she continued to smile anyway and gave him a nod as she sprinted out the door.

Rather than return to the manor, she clutched the letters in her hand and walked through the village. When she found a bench near the fountain, she sat and held the papers in her lap, staring down at them as though they were a foreign object.

It was hard to forget the way Gabriel looked at her with such fury. As though he were enraged by her questions. The look in his eyes—rage, grief, maybe even fear—sliced straight through her. And it cut her to the core. Only the night before they had connected in a way that seemed impossible. And now...now things were fractured between them once more. It hurt.

Turning her attention to the letters in her lap, she opened the first one from the Tribune. It started with *I regret to inform you* and ended with apologies. The second letter was much the same but with a harsher tone. *I wouldn't work in that horrifying manor if it was the last job on earth.* And the last was nothing more than a simple *no, thank you*.

Nothing could have prepared her for that amount of rejection.

Now, she was faced with her aunt's letter, saving it for last. Gods, she wished she could leave it sealed. But she knew she had to open it. Sliding her thumbnail under the wax seal, she broke it and read the salutation. *My dearest Victoria, how we miss you here in Crown Hollow!*

As she read on, it was not good news. As her gaze skipped down the page of the elegant handwriting, a mixture of horror and dread pounded through her. Her stomach clenched into a tight knot.

I thought it prudent that the Honorable Earl of Berkhampstead, Lord Charles Howard, and I visit your estate. Did you know he's the 22nd Earl of

Berkhampstead? He was quite interested in hearing all about Ravenfell Manor and simply insisted on coming to see it and you. I think you'll like him! He's a very nice man. Handsome with a sizeable wealth and a lovely brownstone in Crown Hollow.

Of course, you needn't worry about us imposing on you. I know full well, from your uncle, the ram-shackle state of the manor. So, not to worry. I have a cousin not far from you there in the country and she'll be happy to host us.

We'll see you in the forenoon on Thursday next—

Oh, gods! That was today!

Victoria leapt to her feet, the rejection letters from the Tribune fluttering to the ground at her feet. She hastily snatched them up, crumpling them and her aunt's letter in her fist.

She sprinted through the village streets, clutching the wrinkled regrets in one hand and panic in the other while simultaneously whispering a fervent wish. *Let Gabriel be in the garden. Let her reach the manor before the knock came at the door.*

She didn't stop even as the silhouette of Ravenfell came into view at the end of the road. It rose ahead of her, dark and looming as it always had, utterly unaware of the storm that was about to crash through its front door.

But as she crested the hill, and the driveway came into full view, she skittered to a halt.

The storm had already arrived.

A sleek black carriage stood parked in front of the manor, its wheels glistening from the road. A footman opened the door as the passengers exited. Laughter echoed on the drive. One of the voices unmistakably her aunt.

No.

Her stomach dropped to her shoes. Sweat dampened her dress and her hair stuck to the back of her neck. She watched, horrified, at what was unfolding before her.

Gabriel stood in the doorway, his face unreadable. His body was stiff, his shoulders square, his jaw tight. Her aunt looped her hand through the arm of the tall, blond man in a pristine coat of dark navy as she chattered away, fluttering her lashes and looking utterly ridiculous.

Victoria couldn't move. The letters drifted from her hand, scattering on the ground, as a sick feeling crept up her throat.

She was frozen in place, unable to take one more step, and thankful no one saw her standing there, terror rising like a knot in her throat.

Gabriel stepped aside and motioned for them to enter the manor. Her aunt tittered something. The blond man—who must be the earl—followed her, disappearing inside. And Gabriel, pausing there in the doorway to glance toward the carriage in disdain, finally turned and closed the front door.

Victoria bent to pick up the letters before they blew away in the wind. She knew she had to face her fate. She knew she had to go into the manor, but gods, every part of her recoiled from it.

Steeling her nerves, she shoved the letters into her pocket and walked to the manor. She pushed open the door, the sunlight slashing across the floor, elongating her shadow. Voices came from the parlor. The faint clank of dishes in the kitchen.

Rather than face her aunt and the earl, she decided to face Gabriel first. To explain. But what explanation could she give him? She knew this arrival was a likely event by the first letter her aunt sent. Her hope was the idea would die when Victoria didn't answer.

In the kitchen, Gabriel prepared a tea tray. When he heard her enter, he spun to face her.

Fury was written all over his face.

It made her shrink away. To step back. Facing her aunt did not seem so daunting now as she and Gabriel stared each other down.

"Did you know?" His voice was hard as stone.

"I-I..." She dragged in a breath, ragged and unsteady, and started again. "Aunt Eloise mentioned she wanted me to meet someone, but I never thought she'd come here."

"And that someone being this man who has invaded my house."

She blinked, unsure how to respond to that. Then her own fury boiled. "*Your* house? I believe Ravenfell is my inheritance. And I never wanted her to come here. I only received the letter this morning. She must have posted it after she sent the first. I would have told you beforehand, but they were already here."

His jaw clenched as he turned away to remove the boiling kettle from the stove. "They can't stay."

"They aren't." She clenched her fists.

"They want to stay for luncheon."

This sounded like an affront. As though their visit and demand to remain for luncheon was an imposition. Perhaps it was. The house hadn't welcomed guests in years. She wondered how long it would tolerate this visit.

His hands worked in methodical movements as he poured the boiling water in the teapot. She watched as he placed cups, creamer, and sugar bowl on the tray, then picked it up.

"Gabriel, I'm sorry."

"So am I."

He said nothing else as he brushed by her and exited the kitchen.

Following him was her only option. She headed out of the kitchen, across the foyer, and into the parlor where her aunt chattered endlessly about nothing. The earl sat on the edge of a chair, a tight smile on his face. Gabriel placed the tea service down on the low table just as Victoria entered the room.

"Ah, there you are! My dear, where have you been hiding?"

Her aunt rose from her position on the sofa and bustled toward her, giving her a once over. Clearly, she did not approve of the state of her gown. Faint grass stains were on the skirt where she had kneeled in the cemetery. Sweat dampened her bodice and back and her hair was disheveled and not at all tidy. She was not presentable enough to receive guests.

"My goodness. Are you well? You look flushed," her aunt said.

She looked at Gabriel who shot her a glare as he stepped out of the room, disappearing in the depths of the manor. His presence was the only thing that gave her strength and now he was gone. Leaving her alone with the wolves.

"I...I got your letter today saying you were coming. I hurried from the post," Victoria said. "I apologize for my appearance. I should change."

"No need on my account," the earl said, rising from his chair. He stepped around her aunt and offered her a brilliant smile.

He *was* handsome with striking blue eyes, blond hair that swooped across his forehead, a perfect face that exuded aristocracy. Indeed, he looked how the 22nd Earl of Berkhampstead *should* look. Regal. Noble. Finely dressed. He exuded old money.

"It's a pleasure to meet you," he said.

"Oh, how impertinent of me!" her aunt gasped. "Lord Charles, this is my niece, Miss Victoria Ravenwood. Victoria, darling, may I present to you the Earl of Berkhampstead?"

"Nice to meet you," she said, stiffly.

He extended his hand to her. She took it, reluctantly. His fingers closed around hers, giving her a strong, hearty handshake.

"Your aunt has told me a lot about you and this manor." He glanced up at the rafters, as though he were impressed by the aged coffered ceiling.

"Has she?"

"Indeed, I have," she announced and stepped to the tea service with a swish of voluminous skirts. "I told him all about your inheritance and how you were left this crumbling pile of bricks *and* the fortune to fix it. Such an exciting challenge for a young lady, don't you think?"

Horror sliced through her as her gaze snapped to her aunt. She sucked in a quiet breath, trying to decide how to respond and what to say. How could Aunt Eloise divulge such personal information? Her aunt prattled on, unaware of her misstep, as she poured a cup of tea.

"I really don't understand how you can stay here with that...that...caretaker." She gave a mock shudder and wrinkled her nose in disdain. "So cold and aloof. How do you two get on?" She turned her prying gaze on Victoria, clearly looking for gossip.

"We get on just fine," Victoria said, tersely.

Next to her, the earl shifted, uneasy. He cleared his throat.

"I understand your mother planted most of the gardens with prize winning flowers," he said, trying to steer the conversation a different direction. "I'd love to see them."

"Oh—" Victoria began.

The clink of a cup on a saucer interrupted her. "Yes! Let's see the gardens. It will give us something to do to pass the time while we wait for luncheon to be served."

Victoria tried not to bristle at that. As though Gabriel were nothing but a servant here to take care of every whim from luncheon to serving tea. He was much more than that. She looked from her aunt to Lord Charles who appeared to be uncomfortable with her aunt's brash tone.

"If you'll follow me, then, my lord."

Victoria led them from the parlor, thankful to be out of the stifling room. She hadn't realized just how much she was on edge. A gust of icy air swept through the corridor ahead of them. Too cold for the warmth of the day. Victoria tensed. Lenore hadn't made an appearance, but the manor *had* noticed the intrusion.

And it did not take kindly to their arrival.

Chapter 20

Aunt Eloise hurried along the footpath ahead of them, as though she were intent on giving them some privacy yet remaining within earshot. Likely to interject at any opportune moment. Lord Charles walked next to her in amicable silence as they headed into the vibrant gardens, the afternoon breeze lifting the hair off her sticky neck. A welcome reprieve.

A flapping overhead caught her attention. She glanced up in time to see the raven wing through the air ahead of them. Neither Lord Charles nor her aunt noticed it, yet.

"It's quite the estate, Miss Ravenwood. Though I daresay it needs a strong hand to restore it. Perhaps two?" He gave her a sideways look, one corner of his mouth lifted in a half-grin.

She knew where this was going and she didn't like it. She needed to head him off before he started proposing marriage. "The manor's bones are indeed strong, but I'd rather not tear it down just to make it fashionable."

He paused at a hedgerow, admiring the impeccable trimming. "I have a keen interest in architecture. Especially these old country houses. They simply don't build them like this anymore. But with the right investment, Ravenfell could shine again."

She didn't like his prodding, but tried to maintain her composure. She clasped her hands. Before she could respond, Aunt Eloise spoke.

"Isn't it romantic? An old manor, a lady, and a willing suitor. One could write a novel!" She grinned, proud of herself as she paused to sniff a rose.

It took everything within Victoria not to roll her eyes and groan. Lord Charles seemed to take it all in stride.

"I must confess, you aren't what I expected at all," he said.

"Oh? And what is that?" she asked, trying hard not to be offended.

"More timid, I suppose. But you don't seem fearful of a bit of mystery, do you? And this place holds quite a lot of it." He glanced up at the imposing structure of the house behind her.

She forced a smile. "Mystery is part of the charm, isn't it? But I've found some doors are better left unopened."

He chuckled at that, as though she were making a jest. He continued his pressuring ways. "You know, with some funding and the right masons, this could be something extraordinary again. I could put you in touch with my architect."

"That won't be necessary." She kept the tight smile on her face as she shifted from one foot to the other. Would he never give up?

"I only mean to help. Your aunt tells me you're quite independent, but independence doesn't mean solitude. A partnership can be quite fortuitous."

No, he wasn't going to give up.

Before she could bite out a retort, Aunt Eloise said, "Isn't he thoughtful, dear? He's simply brimming with ideas for the manor. Imagine it! Ballrooms, dinner parties, guests. Maybe even a *wedding*." She looked positively pleased at the very idea of planning a wedding.

Victoria suppressed the groan as her stomach clenched with unease. This was all about pushing them together and perhaps him getting his hands on the manor. The surprise visit. His invasive offers of help. Pushy, pushy, pushy.

The raven dove from the sky, squawking as it landed on a nearby tree limb. She started walking again, trying to ignore it. But even so, chills danced up her spine at the significant presence of the bird.

Aunt Eloise had continued down the path toward the hydrangeas. Lord Charles fell in step next to her.

"I apologize if I made you uncomfortable," he said then, his voice low so her aunt could not overhear.

"I'm afraid my aunt has rather high expectations for me." She gave him a weak smile. "I do enjoy my solitude, despite what you may think or my aunt told you. And, truthfully, the manor doesn't like strangers."

It was a lie, but a kind one. If she were being honest, she'd say she liked her solitude *with Gabriel,* who was now furious with her. How she was ever going to mend the relationship with him, she didn't know.

That seemed to interest Lord Charles. He cocked his head to one side and cast a glance at her. "Do you mean to tell me it sulks when someone tries to fix its roof or freshen the paint?"

A sudden chill prickled the air. She stopped walking and looked up. The raven had flapped to another limb ahead of them and cawed.

"Oh! Ghastly thing. Must be some local omen. You don't believe in such nonsense, do you, Lord Charles?"

"No, madam, I don't."

"I do," Victoria whispered. Because she'd seen what happened in the manor firsthand when Lenore was upset.

"What a glare it's giving us," Lord Charles said, sounding amused. "As though I've trespassed on sacred ground."

"Perhaps you have," Victoria replied, tersely.

"Are you telling me this manor has a guardian with wings?" He chuckled.

"It's a warning," Victoria said.

"Oh, Victoria, honestly! Next you'll say it speaks in riddles," Aunt Eloise said with a laugh.

Nevermore.

The whispered word whistled through the trees. A sudden fog churned around their ankles. And Victoria knew it was time to return inside the manor. The raven let out a harsh croak before fluttering to another nearby branch.

"I should have brought breadcrumbs. I seemed to have offended your guardian," he said with a laugh.

He didn't know the half of it. Victoria turned back the way they came. "Perhaps we should go inside. I'm sure luncheon is ready to be served."

She needed to usher them off the path and quickly, before something dreadful happened. She thought of the shattered greenhouse and the hiding gravestones and needed out of this garden.

"Perhaps you're right," Lord Charles said.

"Yes," Aunt Eloise added. "I'm quite famished."

As they walked back to the manor, though, dread coiled low and hot in Victoria's gut.

Once inside, she led them to the dining room where Gabriel had already set the table. The rattling of dishes in the kitchen was the only indication he was nearby. Lord Charles held her chair for her, then her aunt, then took the seat opposite them. Aunt Eloise examined the room with a critical eye. Victoria braced herself.

"I forgot how charming this room is. The last time I was here was at a dinner party your parents hosted," she said, placing her napkin in her lap. "Could use a renovation though. It feels ghastly archaic."

Victoria ignored the barb and focused on something the woman said. Her aunt had never mentioned being here before. "I didn't realize you'd visited."

"You lived here before?" Lord Charles asked.

"Yes, when I was a child," she replied.

At that moment, Gabriel entered to serve the soup—parsnip and thyme in porcelain bowls garnished with a drizzle of spiced oil and black pepper. He left a loaf of rustic brown bread in the center and disappeared to the kitchen without a word.

Victoria had tried to catch his gaze, but he avoided her like she had the plague. She picked up the soup spoon.

"I hadn't realized you lived here before," Lord Charles said. "What was that like?"

There was nothing she wanted to share with him about that experience. He wouldn't understand she saw Gabriel lurking through the west wing, or the ghastly apparition of the little girl she now knew was his daughter.

"It was a long time ago, my lord, and I was very young. I'm afraid I don't remember much," she replied.

But Aunt Eloise couldn't wait to add her thoughts. "Her father was a foreign envoy to the crown. Always traveling abroad. Diplomatic dinners, extravagant galas, and the like. Why, my poor sister barely had time to unpack her trunks before they were off again! Of course, this was after they'd left Ravenfell. Before that, they spent several years here shortly after Victoria was born. That's when Eleanor started planting her garden."

Victoria stiffened at the way she spewed the information as though it were nothing more than common knowledge.

"I believe my father knew yours, Miss Ravenwood," Lord Charles said.

"Oh?" The word came out on a breath as she sat, frozen. Her stomach clenched tight. Her appetite gone.

"Your father was quite the statesman, you know. My father spoke very highly of him. He often said how he had a knack for turning enemies into allies with nothing more than a vintage glass of port." He dabbed the corners of his mouth with the napkin before pushing away the soup bowl.

"He never talked about his work," she said.

Gabriel entered then to clear away the dishes and place the next course. Poached pheasant in a red wine reduction with roasted root vegetables. As he placed it in front of her, she peered up at him in the hopes she would catch his gaze. But no. He turned away immediately and placed a plate in front her aunt, then moved to the earl.

The way he ignored her cut her to the bone.

She picked up her fork and started to dive in when it struck her how the dark sauce pooled like blood on the plate. She put down her fork, her stomach queasy.

Lord Charles continued as though there was no interruption. "He was discreet, of course. All good diplomats are. My father admired him. Called him a gentleman of rare conviction."

But was he? It suddenly struck her as she sat there listening to Lord Charles ramble on about her father that he was the one who was interested in Lenore Blackmore. She recalled the letter she found in the study urging him caution in the investigation, which made her wonder if he knew about the death of the woman and the child in the manor and he was looking for answers.

Just like she was.

How was it, though, he never knew Gabriel skulked along the halls?

"I wish I'd known him better," she said faintly.

"There was talk he turned down a peerage. Said he was better suited serving than ruling. My father couldn't fathom it and tried to urge him to accept. He never did," he continued, slicing through the meat.

"Whatever happened to your father?" she asked.

"Died of consumption," he said. "Just last winter."

"Oh, I'm sorry to hear that."

"Well, I think that's enough of this dark talk," her aunt announced. How she remained silent through the entire exchange was a mystery.

Lord Charles sat back in his chair and gazed at her from across the table, a look of contemplation on his face. "Something just occurred to me. My father mentioned to me yours was looking into an unexplained death. Said her name was Lenore Blackmore."

Victoria's mouth went dry.

"Is that name familiar to you?" he asked.

Before she answered the chandelier over the table flickered. Then swung violently as though someone pushed it. The chain creaked with the sudden movement.

Victoria jumped back from the table, her chair scraping along the floor. She stared up at it, stomach lurching. A penetrating cold threaded through the silence, cloaking them in unease. And she knew then, Lenore had arrived. Or perhaps she had been here all along, listening to their conversation. She struck the moment she heard her name.

"Odd, that," her aunt said gazing up at the chandelier. As though it was insignificant.

Lord Charles' gaze was firmly planted on the ceiling, watching it swing back and forth.

Victoria was about to excuse herself to the kitchen to fetch Gabriel, when her plate lifted from the table and flew straight for her. She gasped and ducked as it sailed over her head and then shattered against the wall. Aunt Eloise shrieked as she shoved from the table and stumbled away. Lord Charles was on his feet, clutching the napkin in his white-knuckled hand.

Seconds later, Gabriel burst into the dining room. Face pale. Eyes wide. Their gazes locked for a brief moment as Victoria rose on shaky legs. Then he stepped toward the shattered plate on the floor.

He didn't need to ask what happened. He knew. So did she.

"My word, what the devil was that for?" her aunt said. "Victoria, if you don't want to discuss your father anymore, simply say so."

Clearly, her aunt didn't understand the calamity of the situation. She clutched her elbows, hugging her arms tight.

"I apologize if I've upset you," Lord Charles said.

But words were not forthcoming. Behind her, Gabriel crouched and picked up the largest pieces. She turned toward him as he rose to his full height and their eyes collided once again. There were so many things she wanted to say and couldn't. Not in present company. His jaw was locked tight for a brief moment until finally his gaze softened.

"It's all right," he said, his voice low.

And then he disappeared back to the kitchen.

But it wasn't all right.

"Eloise, perhaps we should be going," Lord Charles announced then. He rounded the end of the table and took her by the arm.

Aunt Eloise's gaze flicked from him to Victoria. She gave a nod. "Perhaps you're right. My goodness, it's cold in here."

But as they passed out of the dining room, Victoria caught a glimpse of Lord Charles' grim expression. As though he suspected what had happened but said nothing.

The moment they were out of the room, the chandelier stilled.

A warning.

And then Lenore was gone.

Chapter 21

Victoria remained where she stood, unable to move, as she watched them leave. Moments later, the front door opened and closed with a snap.

Silence descended.

She heard the clink of dishes in the kitchen. Gabriel emerged carrying a broom and dust pan. They stared at each other for a long moment, as if separated by a vast ocean neither could traverse. The distance felt wide and un-crossable.

Victoria moved aside to allow him to clean up the remaining pieces of the shattered plate. She hated this dissonance between them and searched for a way to smooth things over with him.

"Gabriel—"

"This is what happens when strangers enter the manor." He scooped the remaining shards of porcelain into the dust pan.

"I didn't know until it was too late."

"They cannot return." His voice was hard as he turned and headed into the kitchen.

Anger flared bright and hot through her. She followed, shoving open the door. "And how am I supposed to keep them away?"

He tilted the dust pan into the trash, the shards leaving a tinkling sound behind. "I couldn't say. But if they return, things will get worse."

"She is my aunt. My mother's sister. The only family I have left. I cannot simply forbid her to return." Victoria clenched her hands into fists, a hot wave of fury rising through her like a tide threatening to crash.

Gabriel turned away from her, refusing to look at her, as he leaned the broom against one of the cabinets. He picked up a bowl and poured out the remaining soup, as though she hadn't spoken.

"Gabriel, look at me."

Her demand was met with cold silence. He replaced the bowl and picked up another one. In a fit of rage, she moved to him, jerked the bowl out of his hand and dropped it in the trash. He started to protest, his face turning a pale shade of red, when she clutched his hands. Stunned, he froze, his eyes pinned on hers.

"I know what's happening but I don't know why. Tell me."

He jerked his hands free and turned toward the sink. "No. You wouldn't understand."

"Maybe I will," she insisted. "I know your wife and child died here, but I do not know why or how you are still here. I know I saw you when I was a child. Did my parents see you? Did they know you were here?"

He said nothing. His back stiffened, the muscles going taut across his shoulders. He would not meet her eyes. She forged on, trying to put the pieces together.

"Lenore's spirit is restless. She haunts this place, doesn't she?" she asked. Still nothing. "My father was searching for answers. I think he knew. I think he was close to the truth. Is that why we had to leave? Why we—"

"Enough!"

He spun to face her, fury etched on his features. She had never seen him this way before. Never felt the anger and the despair emanating off him in heated waves.

"If you are going to leave and return to the city, Miss Ravenwood, then perhaps you should do that tonight," he said.

And then he stomped out of the kitchen, the door swinging shut in finality. In that instant, her heart shattered.

The letter she intended to post to her uncle was still in her pocket. But she didn't need to announce her arrival, did she? Her uncle would understand something had changed if she simply appeared on his doorstep.

Victoria fled from the kitchen, up the stairs, to her room. She paused there in the doorway, scanning the contents of her life. When she first arrived, she thought this was a fresh start. A way to put the past behind her. Instead, the past continued to haunt her and follow her every step through the manor.

She didn't need any of these things. They were just *things*. And with her inheritance, she decided, she'd buy a new wardrobe once she returned to the city. She'd stay with her aunt and uncle until her aunt managed to marry her off. Perhaps to Lord Charles, which made her shudder.

Turning away from her room, she paused in the hallway, staring down at Gabriel's room. Door shut. Then glancing at the west wing, shrouded in shadows and mystery.

With her gut twisted into a knot, she headed down the stairs, her hand on the banister. She did not know where Gabriel was in the house nor did it matter.

She stepped off the stairs and halted there, giving the house one last glance.

"I'm leaving," she announced, unsure if Lenore was listening. Suspecting she was. "And I won't be coming back."

As she moved toward the front door, the warmth was gone. Cold tendrils wrapped around her. She squeezed her eyes shut.

"Please, Lenore," she whispered. "Please, let me go."

Nevermore.

Victoria tried the knob. It wouldn't budge.

There was an exit off the kitchen at the back of the house. She'd leave that way. She turned to head toward the dining room. As she approached, the door slammed shut. The walls rattled. She spun away, looking for signs of life. Of Lenore.

"You can't keep me here," she said. "I'm not your prisoner."

The cackled laugh echoed through the halls.

She ran toward the foyer once again, skittering to a halt near the front door. Across from her, the parlor. Fog poured from the room. The piano played an eerie tune. She thought for sure she heard Lenore's voice.

You cannot leave.

With her pulse pounding rapidly, she walked toward the parlor. Her nerves on edge. She stepped inside the threshold and halted, peering inside. The fog persisted. The music continued. And there, sitting on the bench, playing the piano was an apparition.

The ghostly face turned to look at her, eyes the color of ink meeting hers. Dark locks spilled down her back and over her shoulders. Victoria recognized her as the young woman from the portrait.

This was Lenore.

She had finally made an appearance.

Victoria sucked in a breath, blew it out. It fogged. Lenore continued to play that haunting tune. Continued to look at her with those dark, baleful eyes.

She could not stay here another moment. She spun toward the door.

It slammed shut in her face.

Victoria tried the knob, but it wouldn't budge. The laugh behind her sent chills up her spine. She pounded on the door, crying out for Gabriel.

He can't help you. Just like he couldn't help me.

That voice wrapped around her, sending cold tendrils of fear through her.

She beat on the door until her fist ached. "Gabriel!"

Then, the music stopped, and the voice was no longer a whisper. "He can't hear you."

A shudder went through her as she turned, slowly, to face the specter before her. Lenore rose from the bench and hovered above the ground. Floating there. Looking at her as though she were a pox upon the household. Victoria backed up, banged against the door as the woman approached her.

"You think to leave this place." Her words rasped in a roughened whisper. "You cannot. You're part of it now. You're part of the bloodline."

The elegance of her face twisted into rage as she lunged forward.

Victoria screamed as something flared bright and hot inside her. Lenore's ghostly face contorting in pain was the last thing she recalled before the darkness took her.

Chapter 22

Gabriel retreated to his room, slamming the door with a finality that seemed earned.

He raked his hands through his hair and peered at his hollowed face in the full-length mirror of his dressing room. Shadows smudged under his eyes as the war within him continued to rage.

He couldn't tell Victoria the truth. Couldn't let her see what he truly was. Couldn't allow his carefully built façade to crack.

Because she was closer to figuring out the truth. She was putting the pieces together. It was only a matter of time before she found out why her father was here searching for answers. Why her father insisted he remain hidden where no one would see him.

But *she* had seen him. From the first night she'd spent in this house, she knew he was there.

He'd seen her vulnerability even then, when she was small. And her sweetness. Victoria did not yet remember the moment he saved her. She was seven, perhaps eight. It was shortly before the Ravenwood's packed up and left the manor.

He stood at his window and saw her walking through the gardens. Somehow, she'd wandered out alone, perhaps looking for her mother who spent many hours there cultivating her flowers. She wasn't supposed to be there. She'd started for the path to the hidden graves.

And she was not alone. Lenore was there, too. Drifting like smoke along the hedges, her watchful eyes on the girl.

Something ancient and knowing tightened in his chest.

Gabriel moved before he could think. He dashed down the stairs, made it through to the back door unseen, unheard, and into the gardens. The girl was poised at the side of the abandoned gravel path, caught in a trance. Lenore was nearby, ready to take her and drag her to that awful place under the tree.

If my daughter is not allowed to live, neither is hers.

The words rang out in Gabriel's head. Not spoken aloud, but pressed into the air. Cold. Final. A curse born of grief and rage.

Revenge. Spite. She wanted to steal Victoria away from her mother, as death had stolen Lenore's own child.

He saw Lenore's hand reach for her shoulder, saw the shimmer of magic begin to form.

Gabriel launched forward. His hand landed first.

The spell broke. She blinked and turned her youthful face up at him with wide, startled hazel eyes. Her face was pinched with confusion.

"You're the man in the west wing," she whispered.

He hadn't answered as he knelt before her, shielding her from the presence of the ghost. Lenore hissed her frustration, then vanished into the fog.

Victoria ran past him, heading for the house, leaving him there alone. He remained, wondering why his chest suddenly felt hollow, why he suddenly felt weak.

A clamor downstairs broke him free of his thoughts. He thought he heard shouting. His brows drew together as he hurried toward his bedroom door and tried to pull it open.

It didn't budge.

Then he heard the faint piano music lilting through the house. A mournful tune. Lenore's tune. And he knew he had to get to Victoria.

He jerked on the door, yanking hard until it came free. The moment it did, he heard her scream.

Gabriel dashed down the stairs. At the foot, he saw the parlor door shut. He went to it immediately, pulled it open. And there, crumpled on the floor, was Victoria.

"Oh, gods. Victoria!"

He dropped to his knees next to her, reaching out a hand to hers. Her skin was cold and clammy. Her face was pale. Her eyes closed.

Without hesitation, he scooped her up into his arms and headed for the sitting room where they had waited out the storm and he talked about books. As though they were a normal, every day couple.

But they weren't, were they? And this time, he wasn't there to shield her from the malevolent ghost. But he didn't put her down on the settee. He cradled her against him, holding her close, trying to warm her chilled body with his.

He admonished himself for not being there. For not keeping watch over her. He wasn't fast enough. He wasn't strong enough. Just like before.

He could lie to her. He had. More than once. But every time she looked at him with those innocent eyes, something inside him cracked a little wider. Chipping away at his resolve. If she ever learned the truth, she would never forgive him.

She shifted in his arms and let out a breath. Her hand slid to his collar, fingers curling there, as if to signal she was all right as long as he held her. He blew out a breath he hadn't realized he was holding.

"I should have been there," he whispered.

Gabriel pressed his cheek to her forehead. She was so cold, as though the ghost had drained the warmth from her very soul. He held her tighter, determined to give it back. He felt Lenore's presence linger. Thin, angry, full of malice. But he did not flinch.

"Go away," he whispered. "Haven't you done enough?"

A beat of silence, then the room warmed again and the presence of Lenore was gone. He clutched Victoria to his chest, leaning back into the cushions and holding her while she slept. It didn't matter if she stayed that way the rest of the day.

He wasn't letting go. Not this time.

Victoria came to her senses slowly. The first thing she was aware of was Gabriel's arms wrapped around her in a tight embrace. The second was that she appeared to be cradled on his lap.

How in the gods had that happened?

Then it came back to her. The parlor. The mist. The piano.

Lenore.

Her eyes blinked open, but she remained still. She heard his deep, rhythmic breathing. The slow rise and fall of his chest against her ear.

He slept.

And yet, his arms did not relax.

Her hand rested against his chest. His warmth. His fingers were curled around hers, holding her, as though afraid she might escape. With him, she had a sense of safety and security. Even though they were at odds earlier that day, even though he was angry with her, here he was. Holding her.

Without moving, she used her senses to figure out where they were. Not her room. Or his. The sitting room. Where they'd stayed together to wait out the storm and he'd told her about his favorite books. That he liked stories of high adventure with pirates. And she'd told him about the death of her parents. When she had, it was like a weight had lifted. To be able to share it with someone else was a balm to her tattered soul.

The shadows were deep inside the room. As though only one lone candle flickered, casting a pale yellow glow. What time was it? The last thing she recalled was it was early afternoon after the horrible luncheon with her aunt and Lord Charles. And then...the parlor.

She shifted then, unable to hold still any longer.

He startled, his fingers twitching against hers before releasing her. She slipped out of his grasp and settled on the settee next to him, putting distance between them on the velvet cushions. He looked at her with his sleepy-eyed gaze. Confused at first, then clarity came back into his eyes. He started to reach for her, then pulled back his hand.

"Are you...are you all right?" he asked, his voice thick.

"Yes," she said.

"Would you like tea?" He rose from his prone position, stretching his back.

"No." She lifted her hand up to him. "Don't leave."

He froze there for a moment, unable to move. His gaze landed on her outstretched hand. Finally, he reached for her, clasped it, and lowered back down to the cushion next to her. Closer this time.

He held her hand for a long moment. No sound in the room other than the faint flicker of the candle on the side table.

"I'm sorry I wasn't there," he murmured. "I should have been."

"It's not your fault," she said.

Gabriel slipped his hand out of hers and rose again. Restless. He picked up a tinder box and walked around the room lighting candles, giving it a warmer glow. She watched his stiff body movements as he struck each match with precision. Lighting first one candle, then the next.

"The room is chilled. I'll start a fire." He replaced the tinder box and went to the hearth, kneeling there.

Victoria remained where she was, huddled in the corner of the settee, watching him. Their afternoon argument played through her mind. Things she said, things he didn't say. She wanted answers. Needed answers. Needed to know what Lenore meant when she said *you're part of the bloodline.*

"Gabriel..." Her voice was quiet in the gloom, drifting across the space to him.

He paused a moment, his hands stilled holding a log of wood. He waited for her to say something, but she didn't know what to say. He placed the wood on the pile and then reached for a match.

"I think..." she started again. "I think we need to talk."

"There is nothing to talk about." He struck the match and lit the fire.

"Yes, there is. There is a great deal to talk about."

He didn't turn to look at her, but she saw the muscles grow taut across his back through his shirt. He tossed the spent match aside and rose in one fluid movement. His eyes met hers. She gazed up at him, the light from the candles reflecting in his dark orbs. His face was etched in concern with a hint of fear.

"I know you have questions," he started. "But I...I cannot answer them."

"Why not?"

He pressed his lips together in a thin line. And then she understood. He was afraid to tell her the truth. He was afraid if she knew, that it would change things between them. Perhaps it would. Perhaps things would be different. For the better. Or perhaps for the worse. But didn't she deserve to know why her house was haunted by the woman he was once married to?

"Tell me what happened in the parlor," he said, pushing the conversation the direction he wanted it to go.

She swallowed hard, looking away, fixing her gaze on some distant space in the room she could not see. Her mouth had gone dry.

"I tried to leave for good," she admitted. "But *she* did not want me to."

"She?" he prompted.

"Lenore." She glanced up.

His brows were knit together in a severe line.

"The front door wouldn't open. And then..." She fisted her hand against her lap, remembering the horrible feeling. "Then there was a...mist pouring out of the parlor. And the music. The piano was playing. I shouldn't have gone in there. I should have stayed away. But something pulled me toward it. Toward...her. And I saw her there. Sitting at the piano, playing that somber tune."

Gabriel's face drained of color, his features etched in disbelief. "You...saw her?"

"Yes. In her ghostly form. Looking at me with those black eyes. Eyes the color of ink."

He swallowed hard, his throat working. He turned away from her, back toward the fire. The flickering light played upon his features.

"There is more, Gabriel."

Though he may not want her near him, she rose and moved to stand next to him. He averted his gaze, keeping it on the hearth.

"She spoke to me," Victoria said.

He stiffened. "What did she say?"

"She told me I was part of this place. That I was part of the bloodline." She wanted to reach for him. She wanted him to wrap his arms around her again and offer her solace. Comfort. She wanted him to tell her everything was going to be all right.

But he didn't. He remained stiff and still.

"Before I blacked out...something inside me pushed back. I think...I think she felt it. What does it mean, Gabriel?"

Slowly, he inhaled a breath, then let it shudder out through his lips. "It means there's no turning back now."

CHAPTER 23

She stiffened and remained where she was next to him, watching him intently. His gaze was solely focused on the fire, the light flickering across his face. It struck her then how handsome he was and how his face seemed to be permanently etched in sorrow with a hint of despair.

Gabriel turned to her suddenly. "Perhaps you *should* return to the city. Go back to your uncle—"

"No." Her tone held a note of finality. "I tried to leave before. The house—Lenore—reacted. *She* doesn't want me to leave. And neither does the house. I'm staying here."

It had crossed her mind to try to leave again, but at what cost? She would lose more than she'd gain, and her heart rebelled at the idea of leaving Gabriel. Something, some tug upon her heart, made her want to stay here for him. And something deep inside her needed to find out why Lenore continued to haunt.

Her gaze searched his, as though looking for the buried answers. Unable to stop herself, she reached for him, took his hand in hers. His fingers had turned cold, even as he stood before the fire.

"If I go...I cannot leave you here alone," she murmured.

A sardonic smile flickered across his lips before he concealed it. "I'm used to being alone, Victoria. Can't you see that? Besides, I cannot truly leave this place." He pulled his hand free and turned away.

"Why not?" she asked, determined to get to the bottom of it. "You followed me to the village that day. You—"

"And I shouldn't have. It took more out of me than I care to admit." His expression was pinched as he lifted his hand and rubbed his forehead, frustration edging through him.

"What does...that mean?" she asked. Her face drained as she remembered that bright morning in the village.

He expelled a heated breath. "Don't you see? I cannot go further than the village because I'm bound to Ravenfell. Just as Lenore is."

Confusion pulled her brows together. "No, I don't see. Why? *Why* are you bound to this place?"

His ire was rising once again, like it had in the kitchen when she questioned him. When she'd tried to put the pieces of the puzzle together. He stepped toward her, took her by the arms, his fingers digging into her flesh. Not cruel. Just firm.

"Please, stop this, Victoria. What happened is a blight upon my soul. I have not spoken of it to anyone and I never will."

"But if I can help you—"

"You cannot! No one can help me. I am cursed to remain here, in these hallowed halls forever. Just as Lenore and—"

He broke off, as though he were about to say another name. The name of the child. *Lily*.

"Lenore and Lily," she said, her voice rough in the silence.

Gabriel released her and stepped away. "Do not speak her name to me. It's too painful to hear."

In that moment, she understood him. She heard the grief in his words. He had never fully recovered from the death of the girl—his daughter. And that, along with Lenore, still haunted him.

He spun away from her and fled the room, leaving her alone with the sounds of the crackling fire.

Victoria remained in the sitting room for a long time watching the fire turn to embers and listening to the creaking of the old house as she sat alone. Lord Charles was right about one thing. Houses were not built like this anymore. Even as she sat there, her legs curled under her, she decided she was no longer afraid. Not of the house. Not of Lenore.

When the fire was nothing more than a red-hot glow, and weariness pressed through her, she rose and moved from the sitting room into the drafty foyer. The house was cold and dark. It was late. Gabriel was nowhere about. Perhaps he had retired to his room for the night, seeking solace and solitude.

The way he looked at her when she'd mentioned the girl's name was like a knife to the gut. It had pained him hearing it. How much time had passed since he'd spoken her name aloud? How long ago had it been since he'd thought of the little girl who was his daughter?

As she started for the stairs, the memory suddenly exploded through her mind. Halting, her hand on the banister, she let it play out. Let it come to her with such clarity it nearly sent her to her knees.

She was eight years old. She'd wandered out to the garden looking for her mother. She wanted to ask her mother if she could let the little girl in the nursery play with her doll. But she didn't find her mother.

The path to the hidden graves was shrouded in mist, calling to her, pulling her toward it. As a child, she did not understand the significance of that. She merely wanted to go down that gravel path—then it was not so overgrown as it was now.

And then suddenly, there was a hand on her shoulder. When she looked up, she met Gabriel's panic-laced gaze. She blinked, tilted her head to the side. The sun seemed to blot out the rest of his features behind his head, but she knew who he was.

You're the man in the west wing, she'd said.

He said nothing as he knelt before her, as though shielding her. Shielding her from what? Lenore? Was her ghostly presence there that day in the garden? She could not shake the certainty he was there to protect her.

She cast a glance upward to his room. Was his reluctance to reveal the truth now his way of protecting her?

Now more than ever, she needed to find out the answers. She recalled the locked cabinet in the study. Gabriel had never offered the key. Nor had he mentioned it. There was something in that cabinet she needed to see, to find.

She headed up the stairs, entered her room, and scanned the dressing table. There—a hair pin. Slim. Sturdy. She snatched it up with trembling fingers and clutched it in her fist like a weapon. Then she turned and crept back down the stairs, every step creaking underfoot.

The study door loomed before her like a sealed vault.

She slipped inside and closed it softly behind her. The latch clicked shut, muffling the sounds of the sleeping house. For a long moment, she stood still in the dark, listening. Her ragged breathing. The soft tick of the grandfather clock down the hall. The ever-present hush of Ravenfell, as though the manor was holding its breath.

She swallowed her own nerves and lit a candle. Its small golden flame flickered and bent as she crossed the room and knelt before the locked cabinet.

With unsteady hands, she bent the pin into a long, narrow shape, flattened one end, and fit it into the lock. The cabinet's cold metal resisted, as if it sensed her intent.

She twisted.

Nothing.

Again.

Still nothing.

She gritted her teeth and tried again, more carefully this time, easing the pin deeper, listening to the faintest clicks within the mechanism. Her pulse thundered in her ears.

A soft gust of cold air brushed her neck, and she startled—turning, half expecting to see someone standing behind her. But the room was empty.

Just the house. Watching.

She turned back to the lock, heart hammering now, and tried again. Click. A soft give.

One more turn—

With a final twist and an audible snick, the lock gave way.

She sat back on her heels, breath catching, as the cabinet creaked open. Dust billowed out. The air inside was thick and still. Untouched.

As if it had been waiting.

With a shaking hand, she opened the door to the cabinet and peered inside. It was impossible to see the contents. She rose and grabbed the nearest candlestick, holding it down close enough to cast the pale light inside.

Papers. A leather-bound journal. Steeling her nerves, she reached inside and scooped it all out. The papers fluttered to the floor at her knees. The notebook landed with the thump on its side.

She set aside the journal and started with the papers first. It appeared to be old letters. Written to her father. She scanned the contents but found nothing of note. She picked up the notebook next. The cover was leather and tied with a leather cord. She placed the candlestick on the floor beside her to untie the book and flip open the cover.

It was a journal.

Her father's.

The first entry was nothing more than a description of their arrival at Ravenfell when she was barely a year old. He mentioned how her mother worried about her falling down the stairs as a toddler.

The second entry discussed the state of the manor. How his father had left it needing repairs. And how he was determined to see the old building renovated while keeping the original charm.

The old chap didn't see fit to keep up with things, it seemed. Now it falls to me. Eleanor is quite beside herself at the idea of spending money to restore it to its former glory. But I've promised she can design the garden however she likes.

She smiled at this, knowing how much her mother loved the garden and her prize-winning flowers. Then another entry several months later.

I sense the place is unsettled. I knew this, of course, going in. The family rumor was that the place was haunted, but I never put too much stock into that. Neither did my father.

She flipped more pages. There seemed to be long spans of time between entries. As though he'd forgotten about the journal and only picked it up when something disturbed him deeply enough to need a record.

I hired an architect to begin renovations on the manor. A highly respected one, too. And yet it seems the house will not have it. During our brief visit, doors that opened easily for me would not budge for him. The west wing was cloaked in darkness and shadow, as though trying to keep us out. The blueprints he left behind have been on the desk, untouched. Yet when I looked at it, the ink has run.

I do believe there is a presence here. Perhaps this house does not want to be saved. Perhaps it's better left to decay in peace.

Victoria paused, staring at the words. A chill rippled down her arms. Her father had felt it too—this constant surveillance, the unseen eyes. He'd brushed it off as superstition...but still, he wrote it down. Her hand skimmed the edge of the page, fingers resting against the ink.

"How right you were, Father," she whispered.

Turning another page, her breath hitched at the scrawl of a new date months later.

I've written to the Chancellor at the Office of Unnatural Matters for more information. What I found...shocking. I daresay I cannot let Eleanor or Victoria into that area of the manor. Eleanor is already beside herself and certain the house is alive. For once, I cannot disagree with her. I've seen things. Felt things. Unexplainable things.

Her pulse quickened. A draft curled beneath the cabinet door. The candle flickered.

She leaned closer.

The Parliamentary Committee on Occult Affairs was disbanded years ago, but I feel now it is time to restore it. There might be something to these old family rumors. I truly believe the committee could help with next steps in this situation.

Victoria sat back on her heels, absorbing the weight of his words. Her father had tried. He'd reached out to others. No one had listened.

She flipped to the final entry.

The Chancellor was no help and so it falls to me to find the answers. And I have. I found the death certificate for both Lenore Blackmore and her daughter, Lily. Lenore died under mysterious circumstances after the girl drowned in a nearby pond. Tragic. The man she was married to—Gabriel? I couldn't find a marriage license on record—was, apparently, her second husband. Her first was Lord Hector Blackmore, who was much older than her. A marriage of convenience. He died a year into their marriage.

After further tracing, I discovered Lenore inherited

Ravenfell estate from her parents. She is, in fact, a Ravenwood. I was able to trace—

Her breath caught in her throat. The candle flared as if reacting to the revelation, casting her elongated shadow across the study wall.

Lenore wasn't just a ghost.

She was part of her blood.

CHAPTER 24

I t was a stunning revelation.

Victoria read the words her father had written so long ago, now in faded ink, over and over. She flipped a few more pages and halted when she found a crudely drawn family tree. It looked as though someone had drawn it while thinking, trying to work out how Lenore was connected to the man who built Ravenfell Manor more than two centuries ago. Someone—perhaps her father—had scrawled the name *Lord Alaric Raven-wood.* He had several children, but there appeared to be two main branches.

One leading down from his son. The other from his daughter.

Over the next three generations, the family line split. Titles and property passed down to firstborn sons or closest male heirs. The secondary line went in a much different direction with one word and a question mark written there—*Mystic?*

Her father suspected, but did not know.

As her gaze slipped down the page, she saw her grandfather's name, Lord Thomas Ravenwood, followed by her father's Lord

Abner Ravenwood. On the other side of the branch, Lenore married to Gabriel.

The two lines had split and then managed to converge again...in her.

Lenore was a distant cousin.

And Victoria had both her blood and her father's.

That seemed significant somehow, but she wasn't sure how, yet.

She peered into the cabinet to see if there was anything else, but it was empty. Then she once again flipped through the loose letters and pages on the floor. Perhaps she had missed something.

Her hands halted when she came upon a copy of Lenore's death certificate. She stared down at it for a long, quiet moment, her heart lodged in her throat. Before she could stop them, the tears came. Mourning the loss of the woman who must have been drowning in grief over the tragic and untimely death of her daughter. She blinked them away furiously and set aside the death certificate.

There was nothing left to find. She'd gone through all the papers, the journal.

She remained there on the floor, her legs numb beneath her, as she processed everything she learned that night. Certainly, Gabriel knew of this, but was unwilling to tell her anything. And if he didn't know, perhaps it was time for her to tell him.

Victoria stacked the papers in a neat pile, picked up the journal, and then closed the cabinet door. Cradling them all in her arms, she pushed herself to her feet. Then she grabbed the candle and headed for the door.

When she opened it and stepped into the hallway, she sensed a shift in the air. Something she couldn't quite discern. She heard the muffled sounds in the kitchen. Heading down the hall, she paused in the foyer listening to the tick-tock of the grandfather clock.

Gods. Morning already. The darkness hadn't lifted inside her, but the light had returned outside. She'd spent the entire night in the study reading her father's journal and the papers she now held.

And in the kitchen, Gabriel was preparing the morning meal.

She glanced down at her wrinkled gown smudged with dust. But she wasn't willing to waste precious time changing. It was now or never, if she meant to confront Gabriel.

Inhaling slowly, she headed into the dining room. He'd already set the table, preparing for her arrival. She heard him in the kitchen, doing the final preparations for breakfast. She smelled the soft aroma of Darjeeling, which was a warm comfort to her.

As she stood there, rooted in place, clutching the book and the papers, he exited the kitchen carrying a silver tray. He froze when he looked up and saw her standing there.

His keen gaze took her in, looking her up and down. Then his eyes landed on hers and paused there. His brows drew together and for a moment, he looked confused. As though he was uncertain what to say to her.

Finally, he managed, "You're up early."

"I never went to bed." Her words were tight and firm.

It was time to stop pretending he knew nothing. It was time to find out the truth about how Lenore died. It was time to make him talk to her.

"Must have been that long nap you took yesterday afternoon." He placed the silver tray on the table, avoiding her gaze.

"Perhaps. I wasn't tired."

If he noticed the items in her arms, he didn't acknowledge them. He poured tea into a porcelain cup, then placed it on the table. He turned to leave.

"Gabriel, we need to talk."

Her voice stopped him, his body rigid as he stood tall, his back to her.

"About?" The one-word answer was as taut as a bowstring.

"I think you know," she said, keeping her voice steady. She was not going to let him out of it this time. She steeled herself, determined to be strong.

"I do not wish to discuss that."

He punctuated that with his hasty exit back into the kitchen.

Saints preserve her, he wasn't making this easy on her.

She charged after him, pushing the door open. It swung closed with a snap behind her. His back was to her as he placed scones on a serving plate. Their thick aroma permeated the air.

"Gabriel—"

"No."

"Yes," she insisted. "I've been patient. I've waited for you to come to me, to tell me the truth while all these things happened around me. Around us. The tree falling on the greenhouse. The cold mist. The piano. Everything. But I know now. I know Lily drowned in a pond. I know Lenore was so distraught with her grief, she did something horrible. Something irreversible."

The last part was a guess. A gamble. But judging by the way he stiffened, she had guessed correctly.

Then she lowered her voice, gentling her tone. "I know, too, something happened to you to keep you tethered here."

He remained where he was, not moving. Not wanting to look at her. "You know nothing."

The accusation was a gut punch. How could he say that to her when she had proof in her hands? She huffed out a frustrated breath.

"Gabriel, I found my father's journal. I read it. He was searching for answers, too. And I know *why* he was searching for answers. Lenore was my distant cousin three times removed. We share the same blood. That's why the house—why she—calls to me, isn't it?"

He spun toward her, his face ashen, his eyes wide and glassy. "That cannot be true."

So, he didn't know. Or if he did, his act was convincing.

"My ancestor, Lord Alaric Ravenwood, built this manor. His children split the bloodline in two. One was on my father's side.

The other was on Lenore's side. The side that dabbled in dark and dangerous things."

Color returned to his face as he realized what she was saying. His lips thinned as anger pinched his expression. "I don't believe you."

"Then tell me. How did she die?"

An unintelligible whisper sounded through the room. Cold tendrils danced up her arms to the nape of her neck. She had come to understand that when that happened, Lenore was nearby.

"I don't want to speak of this," he said.

He started to flee toward the door but Victoria stepped in front of him. "I know you don't. And you don't have to tell me. But I'm asking you...please...Gabriel. Please, tell me what happened to her. To *you*."

His gaze found hers. And in them, she saw the regret, the grief, the *torment* burning through them. She saw that he did not want to tell her anything. He was unwilling to share with her those last moments he had with Lenore, when she was alive and breathing. His gaze flickered to the papers and the journal in her arms, pausing there for a quiet beat. And then his shoulders sagged, as if the weight of the truth could no longer be withheld. As though he was ready to share with her what happened so long ago.

"You were right about Lily. She drowned in a neighbor's pond during a summer barbeque. We thought she was fine with the other children. Then we heard the screams." Slowly, his gaze lifted to hers and in them, she saw the pain still lingering there. "It was too late to save her. Lenore...she was...heartsick. I could not console her. She refused to bury the girl. Said she was afraid of the dark and would never put her in a pine box, alone, in the dark to rot away forever."

He paused here, swallowed hard. "Then Lenore—I tried to stop her. I tried to tell her not to do it, but she wouldn't listen. She was driven mad with grief. She...tried to reverse Lily's death. And..."

"Oh, gods," Victoria whispered. She pressed cold shaking fingertips to her lips. Was she ready to hear the rest?

"It all went horribly wrong." Then, suddenly, he was overcome with his emotions and reached for her. His hands gripped her upper arms, his fingers clutching her tight. He gave her a little shake out of frustration. "Don't you see? She's trying to pull you in with her. I couldn't save *her* then. I can't save *you* now."

"Gabriel, I—"

He jerked her toward him, wrapping his arms around her in a sudden, fierce embrace.

Victoria gasped. The movement was so swift, so unexpected, it knocked the air from her lungs. Her father's journal and loose pages were crushed between them, pressed awkwardly against his chest, but he didn't seem to notice. His body trembled. His grip was unyielding.

What *was* this?

He was warm and cold all at once. Solid, real. Not a ghost. Not a vision. Gabriel.

Her thoughts scattered. She didn't know whether to push him away or bury herself against him. Her hand hovered, unsure—until she found his back, lightly, hesitantly, as though touching a wound she couldn't see.

Was he trying to protect her? Or apologize for failing Lenore?

Or was he afraid he might fail again?

Her heart ached at the thought. That he carried all of this inside him—the sorrow, the guilt, the curse. Alone.

He couldn't save Lenore. He believed he couldn't save her, either.

But maybe he didn't need to save her.

Maybe...she was here to save him.

The window over the sink frosted over. A cabinet door opened and slammed shut. Just as quickly as he pulled her to him, he released her and stepped back, raking a hand through his dark hair.

She wanted to go to him, to comfort him. But she sensed Lenore's agitated presence lurking, swirling, moving around them and between them. As though she were desperate to keep them apart.

"Go back to the city, Victoria. Forget about Ravenfell and me." He turned, tortured eyes meeting hers. "Save yourself."

And then he was gone.

CHAPTER 25

He dismissed her and left her standing alone in the kitchen with her father's journal and the crumpled pages.

It hurt. Sharp and deep, cutting her to the core. She stood there a long moment, staring at the closed door, the air still shuddering from his abrupt exit.

She didn't understand why his rejection stung so badly. She should be grateful for the reminder of what awaited her in Crown Hollow. The security of her aunt's house, a tidy life mapped out for her, a marriage of duty that would keep her safely removed from this drafty, haunted place and its brooding master.

Only the thought of leaving made her stomach twist.

Because despite everything, despite the whispers in the halls, the shuddering windows in the dead of night, the way Gabriel seemed determined to push her away, she couldn't stop thinking of him. Of the grief in his eyes when he spoke of Lenore. Of the way his hands had tightened on her arms, not in cruelty, but in desperation. As though he feared she might slip away before he could save her...or perhaps before he could admit he didn't know how.

A part of her wanted to run. But a deeper, quieter part—the one that had been awake since she first stepped over Ravenfell's threshold—wanted to stay.

Not just for him. For the house. For the restless dead who deserved peace.

She wanted to help him out of his despair and anguish. She wanted to banish Lenore to the spirit world. She wanted to see these halls restored to their former glory.

With Gabriel at her side. Whether that was as his wife or something else didn't matter.

Only one question gnawed at her now.

How?

She didn't know how to do any of that. And she felt lost. Alone.

The bell at the front door chimed. In all her time here at the manor, she had never heard the bell, nor did she know one existed.

Victoria headed to the front door, dropping her pages and the journal on the foyer table. She pulled the door open to find a young man on the stoop, eyes wide and wary.

"Are you Miss Ravenwood?" he asked.

"I am."

"I was told to deliver this to you." He pushed an envelope into her hand, folded and sealed with an unfamiliar sigil.

Before she could thank him, he bobbed a quick bow and scurried off, as though his feet were on fire. Likely he had heard the rumors of the haunted manor and did not want to tempt fate.

She closed the door, breaking the seal as she walked back the foyer table. The moment her eyes found the familiar script, her chest tightened.

Her aunt.

The letter was excessively polite, but there was something sharp beneath the gentle phrasing. Lord Charles had business in Crown Hollow, so they returned first thing that morning. They would not, unfortunately, be making another visit to Ravenfell.

Victoria read between the lines. Her aunt was displeased. Disappointed. And perhaps finished with her.

With precision, she refolded the letter, the weight of unspoken meaning pressing through her. No invitation to return to Crown Hollow. No promise of future visits. A door closed, quietly but firmly.

Her dread of having to face her aunt again dissipated, melting away like Spring snow. Now that she was gone, Victoria was free to make her own choices. Free to seek answers and face Gabriel without her interference.

Free to stay.

She headed to her room where she deposited the journal, the papers, and the letter from her aunt on the dressing table. Fatigue hit her, hard and fast, after her long night in the study. She kicked off her shoes and laid on the bed. Moments later, she was asleep.

The dream came.

A memory, long-buried. Now resurfaced.

Her parents were alive. She was a child again. And they were living in Ravenfell. It was late at night. Her mother woke her from a deep sleep.

"Wake up, Victoria," she said with a gentle nudge. "We have to leave."

"Where are we going?" She rubbed her eyes as she peered up at her mother, yawning.

But in the darkness, there was another figure. Not her mother. Not her father. Someone else. A woman. With dark hair and black eyes. She had seen the figure once before. Then she was not afraid. Now, she was.

Her mother's breath shuddered out between her lips. She gasped, reached for Victoria's hand and tugged her out of bed. Victoria slid out of the bed, her feet on the cold floor. And there, the ghost woman watched.

"Abner!" Her mother's voice was sharp, fearful.

He stood in the doorway of her room, the light from the hallway pressing against his back and making him nothing more than a silhouette. He waved them forward with urgency. Her mother, holding her hand, hurried from the room practically dragging her.

But Victoria glanced back and saw the ghost woman still there. Watching. Waiting.

At the doorway, her father scooped her up and turned from the room. They headed down the hall, to the stairs. As they did, she heard the girl's whimper and looked over her father's shoulder to see the young girl standing in the hallway.

The walls were crusted over with ice.

The fog swirled along the floor.

And Victoria's mother emitted a choked sob as they quickly descended the stairs.

Out the door and into the balmy night. The carriage waited. The lantern lit to light their way. The footman held the door. The driver waited on the seat with the reins in his hands. Moments later, they were inside. She was cradled on her father's lap. Her mother sat across from him. And then they were away. Leaving everything behind.

There was a moment of silence and then her mother said, "I don't care what you do with it. Sell it. Burn it. Tear it down. Just get rid of it. I never want to return."

But her father knew the manor would not suffer such a fate.

Victoria startled awake, bolting upright, her heart racing. It was early evening.

She slid from the bed, her feet hitting the floor, much like that night when they fled Ravenfell for the city. When her mother insisted on disposing of the manor.

But her father hadn't. He'd kept it. She wondered at that. Did he not want to sell it because it was part of their heritage? If he knew the manor had a sordid history, why keep it? And, furthermore, why pass it down to her?

There were no answers to her questions. No one to give her those answers.

As she perched on the edge of her bed, she thought of Lenore. She still did not know how she died.

She glanced at her bedroom door, an idea forming. There were rooms she had not explored. Rooms that remained dormant for years. What if the answer to how Lenore died was somewhere within those rooms? If she found the answer, would it lead her to a way to put the wandering spirit to rest at long last?

There was really only one way to find out.

He was a coward.

He'd left Victoria in the kitchen, sprinted up the stairs to his room, and sealed himself inside. As if that would shut away the terror spreading through him.

Why did he not destroy her father's journal? Why did he let it languish in the locked cabinet all this time? He was a fool to leave it there, ready to be found.

He sat in the chair next to his bed, his heart throbbing a mad beat and his stomach clenched into a tight knot. Slipping his hand into his waistcoat pocket, his fingers brushed the key to the cabinet, confirming he still had it.

Victoria was more resourceful than he gave her credit. She must have found a way to pick the lock. And now, she had all the damning evidence she needed.

Gabriel raked a hand through his hair, blowing out a heated breath as he admonished himself once again. *He should have destroyed it.*

What had Abner Ravenwood written in that journal? He'd never stopped to read it. Only flipped the pages with the careful script. He hadn't read it because he feared what he might find, what Abner might know about him and the ghostly presence of Lenore.

A shudder went through him. When he thought of how close he came to telling Victoria... He pushed aside those torrid thoughts. He couldn't bring himself to tell her. He could *never* tell her.

He tried to stop Lenore from her dark desperation driven by her unrelenting grief.

Tried and failed.

Back then, had he known Lenore was skulking through the village asking questions and gathering information on sorcery and the dark arts, he would have done all within his power to stop her. But it was too late the moment he found her standing over the body of her dead daughter, a bloodied dagger in hand, the black candles burning with an unworldly green light.

Thinking of that now made his stomach twist. He shot to his feet, prowling the room, pressing his hands against the sides of his head as if to push out the ugly memory. And Lenore shouting, *you cannot take my child from me!*

Recalling the cold desperation in her voice made his blood chill. Even now years later.

Victoria was dangerously close to the truth. He tried to avoid her questions. Tried to keep the truth locked deep inside him. Tried to push her away.

But she was getting closer.

He did not know how much strength he had left within him to conceal the truth from her.

What terrified him most was knowing that every step Victoria took toward Lenore carried her closer to death. The ritual had never been meant for her—it had been meant for Eleanor Ravenwood, the blood sacrifice required to break Lenore's captivity.

Now fate had twisted, and it was Victoria who stood in her place.

Now, she was doomed.

CHAPTER 26

T he house was eerily silent, which seemed odd. Normally, there were creaks and groans and other sounds indicating supernatural life. Victoria wasn't sure what to make of it. Fear skipped through her like icy tendrils dancing up her spine as she stood in the hallway and peered down at the west wing.

Shadows clung to every corner, every nook, every cranny. A faint mist hovered over the floor. And the cold air pressed against her. Like a threat.

Or a promise.

Determination, though, was stronger than her fear. Inhaling a deep breath, she forced her feet to move into the west wing.

Her first stop was the bedroom she suspected was Lily's. Her hand wrapped around the knob, and for a moment, she hesitated. She wasn't sure what she'd find in there. The last time she was in this room a mirror appeared and showed her the ghost girl.

"I am not afraid," she whispered, hoping to give herself courage.

Finally, she turned the knob and pushed open the door with a creak.

It revealed the room cloaked in shadow. Undisturbed. Dust clung to every surface. Spiderwebs drifted from the corners like elaborate lace. In the middle of the bed, a lilac. As though it had just been plucked from the garden.

She stepped inside, her heart a frantic beat. She wasn't sure what she was looking for, but something had drawn her here. Moving deeper into the room, she looked for signs other than the lilac. Signs that there was something—or someone—still here.

"Are you my mother now?"

The girl's voice in the quiet startled her. Her heart fluttered into a wild beat as she turned to see the ghost girl standing near the open door. The light from the hallway filtered in, slashing through her opaque form. Victoria moved closer, trying to keep her wits about her as she peered down at the girl with the large, blue eyes so different from her mother's.

For the first time, she noticed the ghost girl's skin was pale blue. Her lips, too. Her gown was rumpled and wet. Droplets of water shimmered on the floor at her feet.

Victoria managed a smile. "I'm looking for your mother. Do you know where she is?"

Lily glanced over her shoulder toward the hall, then looked back. "Her room is down the hall."

The girl must be referring to the suite she'd explored before. When she found both Lenore's and Gabriel's portrait. She forced a smile.

"Perhaps take me there," she suggested.

Lily shook her head, her eyes wide with sudden fear. "I'm not allowed."

But Victoria was not to be dissuaded. "Then perhaps point to it?"

The girl hesitated there as the minutes ticked by. Her gaze darted back toward the hall, as though unsure.

"Lily, I promise you won't get into trouble," Victoria said, sensing her unease.

"You promise?"

She nodded. "You have my word."

"All right."

Victoria followed her into the hallway once again, where the light seemed to fade. The girl took a few steps toward the main suite, leaving wet footsteps behind, then halted midway. She pointed. There was a door to the right. One Victoria hadn't noticed before in her exploration. One that had not been there before.

"Thank you, Lily," she muttered.

The girl turned and bounced away, her image fading away to nothing.

Victoria remained rooted in place, staring at the door, her heart in her throat. She tried the knob. Though it turned, the door didn't seem to want to budge. After several minutes of trying to push it open, she finally put her shoulder into it, turned the knob and shoved with all her might.

With a groan, the door opened.

She released the knob as she peered into the room. Darkness peered back. The air was musty and stale, as though the room had not been opened in years. She took a tentative step, pausing in the threshold. When her eyes adjusted to the darkness, she saw a room of horrors.

An altar in the center, stained with a dark substance that could only be blood. Something rested in the center. A shape she could not discern. Black candles scattered about the room and around the altar, a few burned down to the nub. Strange symbols were carved into the floor, the altar. And next to it, an open book.

Moving closer, she saw the book first on the table. The yellowed pages with faded ink were splattered with circles of long since dried blood. Bile rose to her throat. Something evil happened here. Something desperate. Something dark. Turning, she was close enough to see the object resting on the altar.

A knife with a curved blade. Discarded. As though forgotten.

Cold settled around her. A warning she was all too familiar with. She clutched her elbows, shivering. She had to get out of here. It was wrong to come here. Wrong to look for answers that were better left as secrets.

When she turned toward the door, she yelped surprise.

The woman blocked her exit. She was no longer a wraith. She was fully formed. Her black eyes stared at her with a hatred Victoria felt. Her long hair hung loose around her face. Her dress was tattered, old. Her skin held a deathly pallor.

"What happened here?" Victoria asked, her voice quivering. Her breath pluming.

Lenore's gaze landed on the altar. "It was supposed to bring her back."

"What was?" Victoria resisted the urge to glance at the knife, the open book.

"It failed. I failed. She didn't come back." Lenore moved closer, her gaze fixed on the altar.

The words slipped into her mind, cold and slick. An incantation. To bring back the dead. Her stomach turned to ice, the air thick in her lungs. Of course it had gone wrong. How could something so unnatural ever go right? The thought barely formed before the ghost woman's black eyes lifted, locking on hers with a weight that pinned her in place.

"He tried to stop me," she continued. "He didn't want to bring her back like I did. He didn't love her as much I as I did. Because she wasn't his."

Victoria shook her head. "That can't be true."

"Not his. *Mine.*"

Instantly, Victoria thought of her father's journal—that Gabriel was Lenore's second husband. Understanding dawned.

"But surely he loved her like his own," she tried to reason.

"He tried to stop me. Tried to make me bury her in the dark. She's afraid of the dark."

Lenore slithered closer. The air dropped another few degrees, making Victoria shiver.

"But now the price must be paid. The debt is due. It wasn't supposed to be you. It was supposed to be someone else," she said.

Victoria didn't understand what that meant.

Lenore's face turned from calm and serene to something grotesque and terrifying. A mask of horror as she charged toward Victoria with her hands outstretched.

Victoria jerked sideways, crashing into the wall and knocking the book off the low table. It landed on the floor with a muffled thud. She skirted around the altar, her eyes on the door as she tried to avoid the apparition.

Lenore swiped for her, but missed. She hissed, frustrated as Victoria stumbled toward the open door. The moment she approached, it tried to close but she dove, putting herself in the threshold just as it slammed on her. With a cry of pain, she shoved it open and staggered out of the room.

Behind her, Lenore's frustrated scream. The walls shook. A crack split the floorboard as Victoria stepped into the hall. She tripped. Her ankle twisted, her foot turning over, and she crashed to the floor.

Lenore was on her in a second, snarling. Her icy hands landed on her as she tried to drag her to her feet and back into the room.

Victoria cried out, the pain searing through her. But her voice wasn't the only one crying out in pain. It was Lenore's, too.

With a hiss, she stumbled backward into the open doorway. Mist fogged around Victoria.

"You'll pay for that!" Lenore shouted.

Victoria shoved herself upright, the world tilting around her. She managed one step before her ankle gave out. Pain flared white-hot, buckling her legs. She went down hard, the breath punched from her lungs. Then the jolt of her skull striking the floorboards burst into a shower of stars behind her eyes.

"Lenore, leave her. She's not for you."

The voice cut through the corridor like a blade.

Victoria's blurred vision sharpened just enough to see Gabriel at the far end, a lone candle in his grip. Its flame danced wildly, throwing sharp planes of light and shadow across his face. His eyes locked on Lenore, dark and unflinching, even as the space between them rippled.

Lenore hissed, a sound like steam on iron, before her form fractured into curling shadows. They slid back through the doorway, swallowed by the darkness within. The door slammed of its own accord, the echo ricocheting down the hall.

The mist thinned. Warmth seeped back into the air, though Victoria still shivered.

Gabriel was at her side then, kneeling next to her. It was difficult to look him in the eye with the shame burning through her but she forced her gaze up. There, she saw relief, anguish, regret, fear. A mishmash of emotions that played across his face in the flickering light of the candle.

"You shouldn't have come here." He wrapped a hand around her upper arm and helped her to her feet. "Can you walk?"

"I just twisted my ankle. That's all."

He said nothing as he released her and turned away, heading away from the west wing. She watched him leave her with her ankle throbbing and a raging headache.

"Gabriel, wait." She hobbled after him.

He halted at the end of the corridor. His shoulders drooped in defeat. Slowly, he turned to face her.

"Come to my sitting room," he said then. "I'll tell you every-thing."

CHAPTER 27

He walked toward her and wrapped an arm around her waist. "Let me help you."

Victoria leaned into him, letting him take most of her weight. His body was warm, steady, the scent of cedar and something faintly smoky wrapping around her. Her ankle throbbed, but it was nothing compared to the rapid pounding in her chest.

The closer they got to his room, the tighter his jaw became. His breathing was uneven—nerves, strain, or something heavier.

He helped her to the loveseat near the window and set the candle on the table. Shadows played over his face, softening and sharpening in the flicker. That unreadable expression—somewhere between restraint and hunger—was back.

"Shall I bring tea?" he asked.

"No need," she replied.

"I should have a look at that ankle."

Before she could reply, he knelt. Her breath caught as he slipped off her shoe without waiting for her consent. He held her stockinged foot in one hand, probing the joint with the other. It hurt, yes, but it seemed to be all right.

"Doesn't appear to be broken." He looked up and the intensity there stole the air from her lungs.

She saw desire.

Her breath hitched.

"That's very good to hear," she said, her words low in the quiet of the room.

His hand slipped upward, over the curve of her calf and a shiver went through her. She wasn't sure what to make of that. She *was* sure she could not control her erratic breathing. What was he doing? His touch was not unwanted but unexpected. His gaze caught hers, deep and conflicted.

"Victoria, I—" He broke off, as if the words would unravel them both.

He hesitated. As though the space between them was an eternal abyss of longing. She saw it in his eyes. She felt it, too, as her pulse fluttered. She leaned toward him, drawn by an irrational thought that he was going to finally kiss her. Knowing that's what she wanted more than anything.

Then, he closed the distance between them, scooting close to her. He lifted his hand, his fingers fluttering over the curve of her jaw. The pad of his thumb grazed her cheek. Nothing could tear her gaze away from his. Not the presence of Lenore. Not the creaking of the house around them.

His hands were in her hair next, tangling the locks in his fist. Her breath hitched as he tipped her head back, his lips hovering over hers.

"I waited a lifetime for you and now you're here," he murmured against her mouth.

It was no casual phrase. It was his confession, raw and unguarded—the truth of his heart laid bare at last.

Her answer never came. His mouth was on hers.

A kiss steeped in yearning and regret. As if he'd wanted it for far too long. And perhaps he had.

The house stilled around them. Quiet as though holding its breath. She'd lost all sense of time as her eyes fluttered closed and she allowed herself to feel everything about the moment. His lips moved over hers with a tenderness that belied his inner darkness, banishing everything that had haunted him for far too long. And she found herself moving closer to him, wanting to be nearer to him, to feel him. She pressed closer, palm to his chest, feeling the wild hammer of his heart.

His mouth moved from hers to trace a line along her jaw, down her neck, drawing an unguarded sound from her. Her breath, erratic and jarring, see-sawed in and out of her as she clung to him, keeping him close, refusing to let him go.

"This is dangerous," he murmured against her neck just under her earlobe.

"I don't care," she replied.

And she didn't. She cared nothing for how it would change things between them. Nothing for what it would do to the ghostly apparition that stalked the halls of the manor. None of that mattered now that he held her. He planted one final kiss on her temple and then clutched her to him, his arms encircling her as her head pressed against his chest.

It seemed important to him he hold her. So, she said nothing. Her body relaxed against his. Beneath her ear, the erratic beat of his heart. He wanted this. He wanted her.

She wanted him back.

But she could not envision a life with him. Not the way things were at present.

"Gabriel?" she queried.

"I've long avoided telling you," he said, his voice was low and thick above her head.

"Why?"

"It will change things. You will look at me with loathing and disgust."

He sounded so forlorn, she pushed away from him, holding him at arm's length. His eyes were full of sorrow. He looked away from her, as though he could not stand for her to see him as he truly was—a broken man.

"I won't," she said.

He rose and stepped away from her, standing with his rigid back to her. "You will."

She took a deep, calming breath, expelled it. "Perhaps you let me decide for myself, Gabriel."

He looked at her over his shoulder, surprised at her candor. His brows rose.

"I'm not afraid," she added.

A smile then. One corner of his mouth. She had never seen him smile. "You never were."

She patted the seat next to her in invitation. He hesitated, the silence stretching between them. Finally, he moved to sit next to her. Close. Taking her hand in his, as though he needed her strength. She gave it to him willingly.

"My solitude here...it wasn't entirely self-imposed. Your father knew I was in the house."

The words jarred through her like ice water. "My father?"

"He found me years ago in the west wing. He saw the altar, the remnants of what Lenore had done. He knew I couldn't leave...that I was bound here. He wanted me gone anyway. We argued. He feared I'd harm you."

"But you didn't," she said, thinking of the garden—the way he'd shielded her.

"No. I stayed away. But when you and your parents arrived, Lenore grew restless. She watched you. She hated that you lived and Lily did not."

She listened. Sometimes with her breath held, sometimes with her pulse skittering in horror as he told her of Lenore's first husband, of Lily, of the drowning and death, of the loneliness that came after. Of how her father had found him.

And finally of the night Lenore tried to bring Lily back.

Victoria's stomach turned at the image. The altar, the child, the blood. The desperate, terrible spell. The knife. The curse flung in rage and grief.

When his voice finally broke, she squeezed his hand.

"It wasn't your fault."

He didn't answer.

They sat in silence, the air heavy with all he'd said and all he hadn't. Now she saw the cruel truth—Lenore had cursed him to these walls, binding him in a prison of sorrow so her vengeance could stretch into eternity. And in that moment, Victoria felt the weight of his torment settle over her soul. She would not let him bear it alone.

She shifted closer. "We'll find a way."

Before he could answer, the candle guttered low. A draft whispered through the room. The shadows in the far corner thickened, almost like a figure standing there. There was a muffled rustle of skirts.

A faint, distant laugh—cold as the grave—slid along her spine.

Lenore knew.

"I should go." She rose, but he gripped her hand, keeping her in place.

He looked up at her. The loneliness coming off him was palpable. In some way, she did not want to be alone, either.

"You don't have to."

She shifted. Uneasy. Unsure. "I don't know—"

A lump formed in her throat. A part of her understood he was still trying to protect her. He didn't want her to be alone in her room.

"We can sit here. Together. If you like. I'll bring up a tray if you're hungry." His voice was hollow. Not quite pleading. Not desperate. Wanting. Hoping.

For a moment, she thought what it would be like. To remain here with him, next to him, in his arms. As the shadows lengthened in the room and the house creaked and Lenore lurked. Perhaps it was best if she remained here with him.

Relenting, she lowered herself back to the loveseat. "All right."

Something in his shoulders eased, though his expression remained shadowed. He leaned back beside her, close enough that she could feel his warmth through the thin space between them.

The candle burned low, its light trembling over the walls. The house creaked in slow, deliberate sighs. Somewhere beyond the reach of the flame, Lenore lingered, patient as ever.

Victoria's gaze held to the wavering glow of the candle. Gabriel was right—something in her heart had changed. Not into the revulsion he seemed to dread, but into a fragile, frightening tenderness. A love she had never expected, not when she first stepped into Ravenfell with dread pressing down her spine.

And as the shadows pressed in, she knew the truth. She could never leave him to face this darkness alone. Whatever it took, whatever the path, she would break his curse.

Chapter 28

It was cold in the room when Victoria awoke despite Gabriel's arms wrapped tight around her. He held her that way most of the night. When exhaustion overtook her, she dropped her head on his shoulder, his arm slipping around her. There was a comfort in the way he held her, the way he rested his cheek on the top of her head.

They must have remained that way all night. At some point, she curled her legs to the side of her, snuggling as close as possible. She didn't recall when a blanket had been draped over them. Even so, she still felt the chill of the room.

As her eyes blinked open, she focused on the room. The soft light emanating from the window behind them, trying to press through the curtains. The candle, still on the low table, had burned down and snuffed itself out. The hearth was still devoid of a fire.

The silver tray he'd brought up was still there on the table, too. The tea cold in the teapot. The crumbs littering the plate of cheese, bread, and fruit they'd shared. They had talked long into the night. About nothing. About everything.

And now, in the bitter light of morning, she sat up. Her neck and legs were stiff. Her ankle still throbbed.

He came awake, his eyes blinking open. Confused at first and then when he saw her still there, the light returned. For a moment, there was joy. He was glad to see her.

Gabriel clutched the blanket, ready to push it off, then halted. "Where did this come from?"

"I thought you grabbed it at some point in the night," she said, pulling her fingers through her tangled hair. "Didn't you?"

"I didn't."

She stilled. They both stared at each other in silence. Each knowing there was another force at work. But who? Certainly not Lenore.

A shiver raced through her.

He set aside the blanket and got to his feet, his body stiff from remaining there on the sofa. Neither one of them wanted to acknowledge how the blanket appeared.

"How's your ankle?" he asked.

She flexed her foot. Dull pain lanced through her. "Still hurts."

"You rest there." He picked up the tray. "I'll prepare breakfast and bring it up."

"That's not necessary. I can walk—" She rose. The moment she put weight on her foot, she realized her mistake and sat with a hiss through her teeth.

Gabriel gave her a pointed look. "Stay. I'll be back to get you."

He gave her no other choice as he left the room. Victoria leaned back in the cushion, listening to the quiet of his room, her senses on high alert. There was something different about this house this morning. Something not quite calm. She wasn't sure *what* she sensed only that there was a thrumming wave undulating, ready to crash. Was it Lenore's doing? Or was it something else? Was there some deep-seated horror embedded in the walls only now trying to seep out?

She had the truth now. She knew how Lily and Lenore died. Just as her father knew. It must have been why he decided to leave in the middle of the night. Perhaps her mother sensed it, too, and could no longer tolerate the sinister pulse of the manor. She was willing to leave it all—including her prize-winning garden—to give herself peace of mind.

Of course, Victoria did not know this for certain. It was mere conjecture. But if she put herself in her mother's place without knowing what had happened here all those years ago...well, she would likely want to put it behind her forever.

Sell it. Burn it. Tear it down. Just get rid of it. I never want to return.

The memory of her mother's words came back to her. Her father, though, had refused to do any of those things. They never returned and instead remained in Crown Hollow.

Thinking of that now, her inheritance, she glanced up at the coffered ceiling of Gabriel's bedchamber and thought about everything that had happened to her since the day she received the letter from the solicitor. Was there some hidden meaning in her inheritance? Did her father want her to find the truth? Did he want her to finish what he could not?

Her mind drifted back to his journal. There must be an entry she had missed. She needed to make her way to her room and look at the journal once again.

She glanced at the bed and saw something resting in the center of it. Pushing herself up, she kept the weight off her foot as she hobbled toward the bed to get a closer look.

In the center was a faded blue ribbon. Frayed on the ends. As though it had seen better days. When she picked it up, she noticed it was damp. Her heart clawed its way to her throat. Lily?

"I gave you the blanket," the small voice said.

Gooseflesh erupted on Victoria's arms as she turned toward the voice. Wet footprints led from the door to where the ghost girl stood behind her looking up at her with wide, blue eyes.

"You looked cold," she added.

Words froze in her throat. The girl's gaze landed on the ribbon in her hand.

"You found my ribbon," she said.

Victoria held it out to her. The girl eyed it, then looked back up at her.

"You can keep it."

"Thank you," she whispered. "And for the blanket."

The girl's pale face lifted to her, wide eyes brimming with a quiet yearning that twisted something in Victoria's chest. For a heartbeat, she thought the child might reach for her hand, seeking comfort. The memory of her question—*Are you my mother now?*—rose like a ghost of its own. She had sidestepped it then, thinking it kinder not to answer. But now she wondered if silence had only deepened the girl's loneliness.

A noise stirred in the hall. The girl's gaze darted toward it. "I have to go now."

She vanished in the blink of an eye leaving Victoria standing there holding the damp ribbon.

"Who were you talking to?" Gabriel appeared in the doorway, his face drained of color.

Victoria lifted her gaze to his. "I..."

She wasn't sure how to tell him. She noticed the wet footprints were no longer there. As though they had vanished along with the ghost girl.

"I heard voices from the hall," he added, as he moved back into the room. He halted and gazed down at the ribbon in her hands. Recognition flickered through his eyes. Then he whispered, "She was here."

His hand shook as he reached for the ribbon and slipped it from her fingers. He turned it over, placing it on his palm as he stared down at it. As though trying to make his mind understand it was real.

"She was," Victoria said, finally finding her voice. "She gave us the blanket, too."

His head snapped up. "She told you this?"

She nodded, unable to speak. She worried her voice would shake too much. He slipped the ribbon in the pocket of his pants. A memento. For safekeeping.

"Did she frighten you?"

"No. She's restless."

"Like her mother," he added.

Though it wasn't a question, she nodded. "Yes, but different. I don't think she understands. She...she asked if I was her new mother. I couldn't bring myself to tell her the truth."

Hearing that, pain lanced across his face and she instantly regretted her words. She shouldn't have told him that. He reached for her hands, taking them in his and giving them a little squeeze.

"Victoria..." His words cut off as he pressed his lips together in contemplation. Then, he took a deep breath. "Are you sure you want to stay?"

Worry lines creased his brow as he looked at her.

"I'm staying," she said.

"I fear I may not be able to protect you much longer. She's getting stronger. The house is...changing."

It was something she had sensed, too, and nodded. "I felt it, too," she murmured. She pulled her hands away and smoothed them down her wrinkled skirt. "I think I should change my dress."

"At least let me escort you."

"I think I can manage if I take it slow." She gave him a smile. Not that she didn't want him to escort her, but he certainly had enough worries.

She started to take a step, when he grasped her hand once again. She turned to face him. Deep in his eyes, she saw a mixture of emotions. Fear. Nervousness. And perhaps even love. He lifted his free hand and brushed the back of it over her cheek, a small smile tugging the corner of his mouth. And in that moment, she knew how he truly felt about her.

He loved her. Though he couldn't say it. Not with Lenore lurking in the shadows.

How he fell in love with her, she was uncertain. She hadn't intended for that to happen.

Nor had she intended to fall in love with him. But here she was, wrapped up in her feelings for a man who was decades older than her. A man who had spent half his lifetime with loneliness pressing through him. She might have questioned if he loved her because she was here with him. Because he was no longer alone.

But she didn't.

Because she didn't believe that of him. She believed when he looked at her with those deep, dark eyes there was life burning there. Life and a desperate need to be wanted and loved right back.

She smiled, her heart thudding hard and fast, as she leaned towards him. She wanted to whisper the words to him, but she held them back. Instead, she brushed his lips with hers, then released his hand.

As she limped out of his room, she didn't look back. But she knew he still kept a watchful eye on her.

Chapter 29

It took far longer than she wanted to get back to her room—which was only a short distance from his. When she made it to the open door, she leaned on the doorjamb to catch her breath.

Her room was exactly how she left it but something felt...off. She had the same feeling in Gabriel's room after he left and just before Lily appeared.

She took a tentative step inside, limping toward the bed, and halted. A cursory glance around the room showed nothing out of place. Her father's journal and the papers she retrieved from the locked cabinet were still on the bedside table.

Steeling her nerves, she hobbled toward the bed intent on picking up the journal to see if there was something she'd missed. As she did, a loud crack sounded throughout the room. She yelped as she spun toward the noise. The full-length mirror had a crack down the center.

It hadn't been there before.

She pressed a shaking hand against her raging heart as she stared at the broken glass.

In an instant, Gabriel was at her door. His face flushed. His eyes wide with concern.

"What was that?" He followed her gaze to the mirror. "Did you...?"

She shook her head. "Not me."

Gabriel stepped to her side, wrapping an arm around her shoulders. It helped still her shaking limbs and calm her nerves. She leaned into him, soaking up his warmth.

"Are you hurt?" he asked.

"No. Just startled."

"I'll get rid of it."

He released her and headed for the mirror. As he approached, the broken pieces fell and shattered on the floor. The muffled laugh—that sinister laugh she had come to associate with Lenore—faded away to silence.

His gaze landed on hers. His expression was pinched with a cross between fury and apprehension. They didn't need to speak of what they heard or saw. They both knew. They both understood.

"She's getting stronger," he said, his voice low. As though he was afraid she might hear him.

But Victoria didn't want to acknowledge that. She moved closer to the bedside table and scooped up the journal. Then she sat on the bed.

"It's all right, Gabriel. Leave it for now."

"I can't leave broken glass here," he said and started for the door.

When he was almost there, he turned back to her. He stretched out his hand in invitation. "Come with me."

"Downstairs?"

His jaw clenched, the muscles ticking along the edge for a brief moment. "Breakfast is ready."

Though she suspected that was not the reason he wanted her to come with him—perhaps he felt she would be safer in the dining room than up here alone—she nodded and got to her feet. It was an effort to walk toward him as she favored her injured ankle. When she hadn't yet made it halfway, he dropped his hand and stepped to her.

Without a word, he scooped her into his arms, cradling her against his chest.

"Gabriel, this isn't necessary."

"It's necessary," he replied, a hard edge to his voice. But his face softened as he gave her a weak smile. "Let me do this for you."

She didn't argue. Couldn't. Nor could she deny how much she liked being in his arms. How things had changed between them since their first meeting. She marveled at that.

He carried her from her room, down the stairs, to the dining room. The lovely aroma of freshly brewed tea wafted through the air, giving her comfort. A linen-lined basket cradled fresh, warm orange and currant scones. Clotted cream and jam were in containers next to it. A dish was piled high with toast. Another with poached eggs.

He put her down next to one of the chairs, then pulled it out for her.

"Thank you." She placed the journal on the table next to her plate and took her seat.

He poured tea, then pushed the sugar bowl toward her. "I'll be back."

In an uncharacteristic display, he dropped a kiss on top of her head before heading back up the stairs to clean up the broken mirror.

She heaved a sigh. She still hadn't managed to change her wrinkled dress. Reaching for the sugar, she dropped a cube into her cup and stirred. Then she flipped through the pages of the journal. There was nothing she hadn't read before.

Frustrated, she closed it and focused her attention on the spread of food. It didn't seem right to eat alone. Instead, she sipped her tea and waited for his return.

When he did, he had a dustpan full of broken glass. She watched as he headed past her into the kitchen, heard the tinkling of the glass in the trash, and then he returned.

"You're not eating?" he asked.

"Gabriel, sit with me." She motioned to the chair next to her. When he made no move to sit, she added, "Please. Allow us to have one normal thing in this gods-forsaken house."

A quiet breakfast with him. Yes, that's what she wanted. Without thinking about ghosts or hauntings or evil things. Just the two of them.

He hesitated a moment until he finally took the seat across from her. He poured tea, added creamer, and then sat back in the chair. Steam rose from the tawny liquid. His gaze landed on the journal then.

"Did you find anything?" he asked.

"Not yet," she said.

The quiet moment didn't last long as she thought of something to ask him.

"Did my father tell you how to break it?" she asked.

He shook his head as he lifted his cup to take a sip. Disappointment flooded her. There had to be some clue somewhere to help them figure out how to release Lenore's hold on Gabriel. She intended to find it.

"I don't think we should be searching for that," he said, breaking the silence.

Surprise edged through her. "Why not?"

"Because of..." He placed his cup down on the saucer with a clink. "What do you think will happen if we try to break it?"

Her brows drew together. "What do you mean?"

"I mean, your broken mirror. What else?"

Oh, she understood then. He feared Lenore's retaliation. Though she didn't disagree with him, she could not accept a future of endless war with an angry apparition. She chewed her lower lip.

"I know what you're thinking," he said, then, his voice soft.

"And what is that?"

"That you want to find a way to do it." He fiddled with the fork on the side of his empty plate.

"Shouldn't I want that? Shouldn't you?" Avoiding his gaze, she picked up her cup and took a sip. The tea scalded her mouth. It was way too hot. She placed it back in its saucer.

He was silent for a time as he sat back in the chair, his gaze on nothing in the room. Finally, she heaved a sigh.

"Perhaps you're right," she said then. "We should leave well enough alone."

His eyes flickered back to hers. When he spoke, his voice was low and soft. "I want to be free of her. Of this." He waved toward the ceiling in a gesture that encompassed the house. "But I don't see how to do it."

Not yet. She didn't say it, but she certainly thought it. She merely nodded and broke off a corner of her scone.

He rose then, suddenly, turning away from her. Turning toward the door, as though ready to bolt. And then he halted, turned back.

She watched him, her chest tightening. He seemed so distant suddenly, retreating somewhere she couldn't follow. His hand hovered on the chair back, fingers curling tight until the wood creaked. Shadows flickered at his shoulders, like something tugging him backward.

When he finally looked at her, his eyes were hollow. "If I ever loved you," he whispered, "I should let you go."

And then he was gone.

CHAPTER 30

An emptiness crept through her chest as she watched Gabriel walk away from her. Her mind spun, trying to make sense of his words.

If I ever loved you...

What did that mean? *Did* he love her and he was too afraid to admit it? Too afraid to tell her because he was terrified of Lenore's wrath? Because surely the ghost woman was lurking somewhere. Listening. Waiting for another opportunity to attack.

Victoria wanted to shout for him to come back, to demand he tell her what he meant. If he loved her, he should let her go? Was that it?

If he let her go, did that mean she had to leave this place and never return? He was bound here. He could not leave. Would he spend the rest of his days hiding from her? From what they could have been because he was more loyal to Lenore than to her, a living breathing human?

No, that was ridiculous. He wasn't loyal to Lenore. If anything, he preferred to avoid her and keep her quiet than tempt her wrath.

Everything in her mind shouted that Gabriel did love her. He had shielded her during her youth. Even now, as a grown woman, he protected her from the malevolent forces that lingered through the corridors.

She remained there a moment, trying to get her emotions under control. Trying to stop her mind from spiraling out of control.

It all felt so overwhelming. So soul crushing. She had no answers. No way to break the curse. No way to release him from his torment to give him the freedom to love her as she loved him. And that was all she wanted to do. That and to live in peace in her house.

Her house.

The words clanged in her head.

Yes, this was *her* house. No longer Lenore's. Her presence should be gone from this place. Not stalking the halls. Not tormenting Gabriel. Not trying to terrify her into leaving.

With renewed fury and determination, she shoved up from the table. Her ankle throbbed, but she ignored it as she snatched up her father's journal and hobbled from the room.

At the door, she had to take a pause to catch her breath and close her eyes, steeling her nerves against the pain flaring through her ankle.

She could do this.

She *would* do this.

Gritting her teeth, she made her way to the study, thinking of her father's desk and all the books. It was slow going. When she finally arrived, sweat beaded her forehead and trickled down her back.

The room was cast in gloomy shadows.

She was tired of gloomy shadows and cobwebs and dust. She vowed to reclaim what was hers. Her birthright. And she was no longer going to allow Lenore to control her.

She moved into the room and halted at her father's desk, her fingers trailing along the shiny surface. The parchment and inkwell were still where she left them when she scribbled the frantic letter to her uncle. The desperation pounding through her when she did that was no longer there.

Victoria placed the journal on the top of the desk. Then she turned her attention to the bookshelves lining the walls. Faint light filtered through the window. She lit the candles around the room, trying to give it more of a cheerful glow. But even that was not enough to cheer this room.

Favoring her injury, she headed to the bookshelf to examine the titles. Most were novels. Nothing more than fantastical tales. A few missing spaces between books made her smile. Those must be Gabriel's favorites. One tattered oversized volume sticking out from the shelf caught her eye. She pulled it off and opened the dark gray cover to the first yellowed page. The title was written in an archaic hand in a language she didn't understand.

She moved back to the desk where she placed it on the top and sat. As she flipped through the aged pages, she saw drawings. A raven with words written under it she could not understand. A curved knife like the one in the room with the altar. She flipped another page and froze, her heart clawing its way to her throat.

This page had pale brown circles. Drops of blood splatter.

It was like the book in the altar room.

She slammed it closed and sat back, her heart racing.

Was this the book from the altar room? If it was, how did it get here?

She clasped her hands in her lap to keep them from shaking.

Footsteps in the hall made her spine stiffen. Then his voice—low, familiar. "Victoria?"

"In here," she managed.

He appeared in the doorway, the candlelight behind him throwing his face into shadow. For a moment, he didn't move, as if crossing the threshold itself took all his strength.

"I came to apologize," he said at last. His voice was rough, as though thc words cost him dcarly.

Her brows knit. "For what?"

He shifted, gaze darting briefly toward the closed book on the desk before returning to her. "For...before." Guilt flickered across his face, sharp and raw, before he stepped inside.

He meant before in the dining room. When he practically confessed his feelings for her and then left her there bereft in a sea of her own emotions. Emotions that were on the brink of spiraling. Emotions she somehow managed to rein in before she cracked.

Uncertainty swept through her as she peered at him from her chair. He lingered in the doorway, the flickering candlelight catching the sharp edges of his features.

"Before?"

He pursed his lips, then ran a hand through his hair. "For wanting what I should not."

"Gabriel," she said, slowly, quietly. "My feelings for you have certainly changed since I arrived here. I sense the same from you. But if you're not ready, that's perfectly fine, too. I'm not leaving this house."

He shifted then, clearly relieved. Before he replied, she forged on.

"This is, after all, *my* house, now. Not Lenore's. It's time for me to take it back."

Gabriel's brows winged upward as he walked deeper into the room. "You found something?"

She motioned to the book. "I think this the book from the…" Her breath hitched. She swallowed hard. "…the room."

He walked to the desk, pausing at the side and leaned down to look at the hefty tome. When he did, she caught the scent of him. That earthy, smokey scent mingling with cedar and old leather.

"Where did this come from?" he asked. "It *is* the book from the room."

"I'm not sure. It was on the shelf over there." She pointed to the bookshelf. "As if it was waiting for one of us to find it."

She flipped a few pages. The same strange symbols and writing were on each page. But when she got to the middle of the book, she halted. A folded piece of parchment was in the center as though the owner left it there and forgot about it. She glanced up at him. His gaze met hers and they exchanged the same look of curiosity.

With a shaking hand, she picked it up and unfolded it. Instantly, she recognized her father's handwriting. Her gut clenched into a tight knot as she read it.

The widow's spirit clings because her grief was not buried with her body. She seeks what was taken from her. To sever her hold, the knife must be anointed with living blood, spilled upon the altar. Three times the banishing chant must be spoken, and the flames must not go out. Should the flame die, the soul of the speaker will be forfeit. This I have learned too late.

"What is it?" he asked.

She handed it to him. Gabriel's eyes scanned the paper once, twice. As if reading it again and again would change the words. A muscle ticked in his jaw as he lowered the page with a shaking hand.

"No," he said.

"It's the only way."

He crushed the note in his fist, his knuckles leeching of color. "Don't you understand what this means? It's a trap. Your father must have realized it and wrote the note too late. He saw what it required."

"I know what it requires." She sounded far more calm than she felt.

"Blood." His gaze locked on hers, sharp with desperation. "*Your* blood. It wants you bound to her in exchange. If the flame dies—if anything goes wrong—it will claim you. Do you understand? You won't be released. You'll be trapped here. Just like her."

"What she wants doesn't matter anymore," she snapped, her voice stern and hard. "I will not allow her to continue to control me. Or you."

His shoulders slumped, defeated. Then he dropped the rumpled paper back onto the book. He kneeled next to her chair, reaching for her hands and taking them in his. He squeezed them tight, then kissed her fingertips. Soft and light.

"No, Victoria." The words were soft, pleading. "I forbid it."

Her heart tightened in her chest. "We have to at least try. It's the only way."

As she said it, the house groaned and sighed in agreement. It, too, knew it was time to banish the spirit that stalked through the halls of Ravenfell.

"I would rather endure Lenore's wrath for a hundred more years than watch you take her place. I don't want to lose you. Not like that."

His words gutted her. It was enough of a profession of love. She tugged her hands from his and placed them on his cheeks, turning his face up to meet hers. In his eyes, she saw the fear burning there and something else. Something he wasn't ready to acknowledge but deeply felt.

Love.

He loved her.

And he feared if he allowed her to go through with the ritual a second time, he would lose her to the spirit world like Lenore. Or, worse, she'd free him and become tethered herself to the manor.

"You won't," she said.

The words sounded more sure than she felt. Her stomach had clenched into a tight knot at the thought of what she had to do, what was at stake.

"You don't know that," he said, his eyes still imploring her.

"I don't," she agreed. "But I have you. And you'll promise me that if anything goes wrong, you'll do what is necessary to keep me from becoming like her."

Even as she said it, her voice soft, the candles flickered as though a violent wind had torn through the room. She dropped her hands into her lap and gazed about the room. He got to his feet, his hands clenched at his sides, ready to fight back.

But it was difficult to fight something unseen.

"Victoria—"

"Promise me," she insisted.

She wasn't certain he'd agree. His body was rigid, his muscles tense. His expression unreadable. Fatigue lined his face. Dark shadows smudged under his eyes. He brushed the back of his hand across her cheek.

"I promise."

A sudden swish of air hissed along the corridor outside the door, sharp enough to snuff a breath. Both their heads snapped toward the sound.

The shadows rippled—moving against the grain of the candlelight. Something rushed past the doorway, swift and shapeless, dragging with it a child's broken whimper.

Lily.

The flames shuddered violently, bending low as though bowing to some unseen force. The air grew colder, heavy with the metallic tang of dread. The house shifted, creaking with an unnatural sound.

He shot to his feet. She gasped, the sound snagging in her throat, and stumbled upright, her pulse a frantic drumbeat in her ears.

"Something is happening," she said. "The house..."

"Yes," he agreed. "I thought we'd have more time to plan."

The walls shuddered around them. And that low laugh echoed through the abandoned halls upstairs.

"But we don't, do we?"

She flipped the large book closed and picked it up. They exchanged a look, both knowing the time had arrived. Gabriel gripped her by the arm and helped her hobble toward the door.

It was now or never.

Chapter 31

"We can use what's left of the candles in the room," he said as they left the study.

When they exited into the hall, he paused, his gaze on the floor. Small wet footprints led from the study across the foyer to the stairs where they disappeared, blending in with the runner. And the sound of the child's crying echoed once again. Lily was leading them to where they needed to go.

"Keep going," she whispered, her voice shaking.

Gripping her arm a little tighter, they started again. It was slow going with her injured ankle, but she was determined.

"And the knife?" she asked.

"You'll need that, too." He sounded grim.

As they walked toward the stairs, she started to form a plan. The candles would be lit and ready. She would use the curved knife, slash her palms with the tip, and speak her name. Three times, it said. Three times to free Gabriel from his torment and send Lenore to the spirit world.

And if she failed...she did not want to think about if she failed.

Where the staircase began, a sudden draft stirred, making the foyer candles gutter and flare. They flickered, leaving garish shadows across the walls. In the parlor, the piano played its mournful tune. Somewhere on the second floor, a door slammed. The house groaned.

A shudder passed through her. Cold tendrils danced up her spine.

Lenore knew she was coming.

Hesitation radiated off Gabriel in waves as he stood there in the shadow of the staircase. She turned to him, placed her hand on his arm, and gave him a valiant smile.

"We can do this," she said.

Worry lines creased the corners of his eyes. He didn't object. He nodded and together they started up the stairs. She took one step at a time to favor her ankle. He stayed right with her, never faltering. Never letting her go.

At the top, they turned toward the west wing. Victoria inhaled a deep, cleansing breath. To give herself courage. To give herself strength. To tell herself this was the right thing to do. She would banish Lenore and free Gabriel—no matter the cost.

As they started in the direction of the west wing, the house suddenly tilted. A whoosh went through her, sending her stomach into knots, making her feel sick. She stopped walking and leaned heavily into Gabriel. He clutched her to him, wrapping an arm around her shoulders.

"What's…what's happening?" she murmured.

But Gabriel's gaze was fixed on the hallway ahead. Fog rose from the floorboards. The chill settled over them, making their breaths crystalize. And then—worst of all—the walls began to crust with ice.

"She knows we're coming. So does the manor. Neither like it." His words were soft, as though he hoped not to disturb either of them.

Ahead, small wet footprints appeared on the floor disappearing down the hall.

"Look," Victoria gasped.

"Lily." Her name came out on a choked sob.

Then the little girl's voice, "Hurry."

Gabriel sucked in a sharp breath. "She's warping the house."

Together, they started once again. But the hall stretched unnaturally before them, making her dizzy. Shadows twisted. Doors shifted. She closed her eyes and pressed a hand against her head.

"Gabriel?" she queried.

"We're almost there." His voice was tight with emotion.

Victoria stumbled, falling against him. It appeared the walls were moving, the hall was elongating. And somewhere deep inside the west wing, a deep, guttural snarl.

Victoria whimpered, suddenly regretting her decision to banish Lenore. There was some unnatural force at work. Something she had never seen before.

I have called upon all the darkest forces to aid me.

Lenore's voice rang out. Gabriel flinched and stopped walking as a shudder moved through him. Victoria wrapped her arm around his waist.

"She's just trying to scare us," she said.

"And doing a fine job of it," he muttered.

"We have to keep going," she said.

As they passed Lily's bedroom door, the ghost girl materialized through it, running ahead of them and leaving wet footprints behind. Victoria released her hold on Gabriel and jerked out of his embrace. She stumbled after the girl, hobbling as fast as her injured ankle allowed.

"Victoria, wait!"

"We have to follow," she said.

Sharp pain lanced up her leg as she followed Lily's disappearing form in the shadows of the elongated hallway. Behind her, Gabriel's heavy footsteps. The ghost girl disappeared through the door to the room with the altar.

When Victoria arrived, she turned the knob but the door wouldn't budge.

"Let me try," he said.

He nudged her out of the way, his hand on the knob. He gave it a twist and then pushed his shoulder into it. It didn't move. He tried again. Same result. He glanced at her, uncertainty in his eyes.

"She doesn't want us in there," Victoria said.

Not him. Only you.

Lenore's voice fluttered through the hallway.

But Victoria was determined to continue onward despite the terror shuddering through her. Even so, Gabriel released his hand from the knob and stepped back. He shook his head. Fear glinted in his eyes.

"We can't do this," he said hoarsely.

She pulled in a shaky breath, released it. She reached for him, then, putting her hands on his cheeks.

"*We* can't, but I can."

Before he could argue, she kissed him quickly, nothing more than a peck. Then shoved him out of the way. Her hand landed on the knob, twisted, and then she pushed the door open violently. She stumbled into the dark room. The door ripped from her grasp and banged against the wall.

She was greeted with darkness and no altar.

"What—?"

"The house," he muttered. "It rearranged itself."

"Because she willed it?" she asked.

"Perhaps." There was a rustle of fabric behind her, then he reached for her hand and pressed something in it. A matchbox. "You'll need it."

Victoria turned to face him. "You're not coming?"

"I'm not sure I should." His gaze flickered toward the dark room behind her.

"She wants to separate us." She took his hand. "We can't let her."

A menacing laugh echoed through the room as though confirming Victoria's words.

Victoria tugged him through the door. The moment she did, it swung toward them, banging into her. She yelped in surprise and pain. Gabriel shoved her into the room, stumbling in after her. As he did, the door slammed shut, plunging them in total darkness.

Cold pressed all around them. And then a hand tugged at her skirts. She looked down into Lily's wide, frightened eyes.

"Lily?"

The girl pointed to a second door, faint light spilling through the edges. She slipped through, the wood creaking.

Gabriel stepped closer to her, his body pressing against her to let her know he was there. Giving her strength. Fueling her determination. Victoria squinted in the darkness to see the door. Closed.

The ghost girl disappeared through it.

The door creaked open revealing shadows and strange flickering, otherworldly light. Light that did not belong.

"Come in. If you dare."

Lenore's voice again, taunting them. She cut a glance to Gabriel, who's eyes were fixed on the open door. He gripped her elbow, his hand a reassuring presence. She clutched the matchbox in her other hand as she took a deep breath. Ready to face Lenore.

Before she took a step, he whispered, "Be careful."

Together, they stepped into the room. The altar was there, bathed in yellow-gold light and in the center, the knife gleamed bright, waiting for her blood.

CHAPTER 32

The air in the room was stifling and heavy with the sharp metallic tang of blood and old magic. Black candles surrounded the altar. The first time she was in this room she hadn't noticed the state of the candles. Now, she did. Some were burned down to nubs, while others were coated in a fine layer of dust with spent wicks and dried wax dripping down the side. The symbols carved into the floor and the altar seemed to pulse with a life of their own. As though it were alive, breathing, and waiting.

Victoria froze, unable to move as her determination waned. There was a strange oppressive energy in this room, making it feel dark and terrible. Perhaps because of what had happened here before. She stared at the knife in the center, her nerves jangling as she steeled herself for what must be done.

"We should light the candles," he said. His voice was a roughened whisper.

She lost a quiet breath in the frigid air. A shiver snaked up her spine, and she shuddered.

"Victoria?" His hand on her arm jarred her out of her thoughts.

She shoved the matchbox into his hands. "You do it."

"Are you...?"

"I'm all right," she said, trying to reassure him and regain her confidence.

Now that they were here ready to face Lenore, she wasn't sure she could go through with it.

But she had to. For him. To release him from his eternal torment.

Gabriel's hand shook as he struck the first match. He started on one end, lighting the shortest candle. When the green flame flickered to life, he snuffed the match and then picked it up. He used it to light the other candles along the altar one by one.

When finished, he returned the candle to its place.

The curved knife in the center gleamed. Beckoning her. She reached for it. The moment she did, a sharp pain shot through her hand. A sharp inhale hissed through her teeth as she drew her hand back, clutching her wrist as though she'd been burned.

"What was that?" he asked.

"I...I don't know. Now what?" Her voice shook.

"You are of the bloodline. Now you take my place and I can forever rest."

Lenore's voice rang out before she fully formed next to the altar. Gabriel moved to stand between her and his former wife.

"No. That will never happen."

Her glittering ghost gaze flickered to him. A smile—cold and evil—pulled at the corners of her lips.

Her black gown was tattered with sleeves that hit just below the elbow trimmed in lace. Lace that was tattered and faded. Her hair, wild and loose, was about her face, cascading down in long waves. And her eyes were dark and dangerous and glittering as she looked at the two of them. Lily was nowhere in sight.

"Well, well. It's good to see you again Gabriel. How I've missed you."

When she spoke, the words seemed to echo through the chamber. Gabriel stiffened, his body going rigid.

"The last time you were with me...do you remember what you said to me?" she continued.

"Don't do this, Lenore." His voice wavered.

"You begged me to stop. You tried to pull me away," she continued as though he hadn't spoken. "While my daughter lay here." She motioned to the altar. When she did, Victoria saw the blood running down her wrist from the center of her palm. "It was too late. I lit the candles. I said the words."

The candles. Victoria glanced around the room and saw the black candles flickered their garish green light against an unseen force.

"She was dead," Gabriel said, trying to reason with her. "Nothing you said or did could bring her back. It wasn't going to work."

"It would have worked. You got in my way," she retorted. "You were always in my way. I should have killed you when I had the chance."

With her heart pounding, Victoria dove for the knife in the middle of the altar. She snatched it up and stumbled back. Lenore howled her displeasure.

"Your time is ending, Lenore," she said. She pressed the tip to the center of her palm.

"You foolish girl. You can't end me!"

Lenore's face contorted from the once beautiful one into something terrifying. She snarled as she flew across the altar. Victoria cried out as the ghost woman's bloody hands landed on her, pushing her back and back. Gabriel shouted her name. Lenore's hands clawed her throat.

The force knocked the knife from her hand. It clattered to the ground.

Searing pain surged through Victoria and suddenly she was outside the altar room. The menacing face of Lenore bearing down on her, pushing her out and away from Gabriel.

But something surged within her as she gasped for air. Some bright pulse that seemed to overtake her body. And then Lenore shrieked and flew back into the altar room. Victoria pitched forward, throwing out her hands to break her fall. As Lenore disappeared into the shadows, the door slammed closed.

Sealing Gabriel inside.

Victoria, gasping for air, and lifted her head. Lily was there, standing in front of the door with water dripping around her leaving tiny circles.

"Lily?"

"You have to hurry," she whispered and then she was gone.

Victoria climbed to her feet, her ankle protesting with every movement, and reached the door, but it was locked. The knob wouldn't turn. On the other side, she heard Gabriel's shout that nearly ripped her heart in two.

When the door slammed closed, Gabriel tried to shout her name but Lenore was there. Moving toward him with that menacing look on her once beautiful face. He balled his fist and stepped back from the door. The ominous green light from the candles gave the chamber an eerie glow. One that was otherworldly.

"It's her I want. Not you," she said. "But I'll take you if I have to."

"I prefer you take me instead," he said, defiant. If it meant saving Victoria, he would do it. He would do anything for her.

That enraged her. She dove for him. Her spectral hands latched onto him. One diving into his chest, reaching into him and grabbing onto his very soul. Yanking and pulling with all the hate within her. He cried out with the searing pain, trying to move out of her grasp but she held fast.

As his vision dimmed, and he started to fade away letting her win, the door crashed open. It was quickly followed by a muffled grunt of pain. Lenore released him and shrieked her frustration. Gabriel crumbled to his knees, pain lancing through his legs as he gulped in air.

Next to him, Victoria climbed to her feet, her hand wrapping around the hilt of the knife as she rose. Without wasting a moment, she sliced her palm, then squeezed her hand into a tight fist. So tight, her knuckles leeched of color. She held it over the altar, the blood dripping down.

"No!" Lenore shouted as she fluttered back to the other side of the room.

"I banish you, Lenore," Victoria said her voice low and terrible.

"No!" she shrieked again.

A howling wind arrived, buffeting him back. He leapt to his feet, reaching for Victoria. The walls quaked beneath the force. The door to the altar room buffeted in the wind, banging against the wall with a loud thud.

"I banish you, Lenore," she said a second time, her voice stronger. Another drop of blood landed on the altar.

"*You cannot win*," she hissed. "*It should have been you!*"

Lenore lunged, her spectral hands locking around Victoria's shoulders. Gabriel's cry tore from his throat, but before he could reach her, the air convulsed. Something wild—holy—erupted.

Victoria flared in a blaze of golden-white light. The glow pulsed from her chest, rippling through every line of her body until she was haloed in radiance, her hair catching fire like spun sunlight.

The brilliance seared the shadows, forcing Lenore back with a shriek.

Gabriel froze, his heart stuttering. Terror and awe warred within him. Was she burning alive before his eyes, or becoming something untouchable, divine? He wanted to drag her away, shield her with his own body, but the light was not meant for him. It was hers.

Lenore emitted an unholy, guttural sound. She clawed at her face, twisting in agony across the altar.

"You cannot have me, for I am of the bloodline and this is *my* house. No longer yours. And he is no longer yours to control. Because I love him. And he loves me."

"Victoria—"

He said her name on a choked sob. His heart burned hot and wild beneath his breast. Where Lenore had tried to take him. Where he had almost allowed her to destroy him.

The wind continued to howl within the room. The walls creaked. The air was so cold, his breath came out in large puffs.

"I banish you, Lenore!" A third drop landed on the altar. "Leave this place and never return."

And then Lenore screamed, her form splintering like glass. It shattered, the pieces turning to smoke and disappearing into the air. In that moment, he felt as though the constricting tether around him released, freeing him from Lenore's curse. For the first time in years, a sense of freedom shifted through him. He sucked in a breath, gasping for air as though he were finally no longer under water and drowning.

Gabriel looked at Victoria. Her hazel eyes were glassy, distant. Her face was drained of color. Blood seeped from the cut on her now-opened hand, dripping on the floor in methodical plops.

The wind calmed.

The black candles snuffed out.

The house quieted.

The frost on the walls melted.

Silence.

And then, Victoria crumpled like a rag doll and collapsed.

He tried to catch her, but he wasn't fast enough. Her body hit the floor with a muffled thud. The knife landed on the ground next to her. He rushed to her, scooping her into his arms, his heart banging against his ribs.

"Victoria?" He brushed hair off her ashen face. Gods, she was cold. So cold. "Stay with me. Don't leave me now. You can't. I won't allow it."

"She'll be all right."

The little girl's voice made his head snap up. Lily stood nearby. Small and glowing. No longer wet and dripping. The scent of lilacs drifted on the air around her. She stepped closer, her little hand outstretched to him, then dropped before he reached for her.

"She saved you," she whispered.

"My little Lily." His voice was raw, hoarse. "I'm so sorry."

"It's all right, Papa. She saved me, too."

A shining golden light appeared behind her, beckoning. She gave him one last faint smile and then skipped into the light, as though her heart was free and she was alive again. Then she was gone.

And all around him, the manor groaned, sighing in relief. It was over.

CHAPTER 33

There was pain. And there was warmth.

The pain lanced through her, sharp and unrelenting, making every bone feel fractured, and her head throb like it was splintering apart. Fatigue weighed her down, her body leaden. Like she'd been dragged down to earth and buried beneath centuries of sorrow.

But the warmth...oh, the warmth. It cocooned her like a woolen blanket pulled close on a winter night. Steady. Rocking. Arms cradled her, rocking faintly, clutching her as if she were something precious. Not something. Someone. Someone loved.

Her lashes fluttered, the world a blur of shadow and faint candlelight. Then Gabriel's face came into focus above her—drawn tight with worry, his eyes rimmed red, his jaw taut. The moment her gaze found his, something broke. Relief shuddered through him, softening the harsh lines of his face until she saw his unguarded expression—the wild, aching relief of a man who'd nearly lost everything. Human. Vulnerable. Hers.

"Gods," he rasped, his voice tinged with the edge of fear. His forehead pressed to her hair, his breath trembled against her temple. "I thought I lost you."

She wanted to speak, to soothe him, but her throat burned, her mouth parched. It took all her strength to drag her arms upward, heavy as stone, and curl them around him. He stiffened, then crushed her closer.

Bits and pieces of memory tried to surface—her blood dripping onto the altar, the words torn from her throat, the searing light that had consumed her.

The light. What was that? She wasn't certain. It burned bright and hot, flaring from somewhere deep inside her as it did that first time Lenore tried to touch her, tried to take her. It saved her then as it saved her now.

Then nothing. Only this moment. Only him.

He clutched her, his face in her air, breathing deep. His breath fluttered over her neck.

Gabriel pulled back, brushing his hand over her face with a sort of wonder flickering through his eyes. And he was smiling. She had never seen him smiling. Not like that.

"Did it...did it work?" When she spoke, her voice was thin and papery, but she forced the words out.

For one unbearable moment, she thought he was telling her no, that this was all for naught. That Lenore still hovered and haunted.

That all of it—slicing her hand, saying the words, watching the blood drop—was in vain.

Then a laugh broke from him. An unguarded, joyful sound she'd never heard from him. Half joy, half disbelief.

"It did." A fierce smile lit up the contours of his face, making him more handsome than she'd ever seen him, pushing back the sorrow and the shadows and making her heart trip. "It did, you marvelous girl."

Relief slammed into her with a reckless abandon. Her eyes stung. A lump formed in her throat. She tried to swallow it back, but it wouldn't budge. The lonely, haunted man of Ravenfell Manor, the one who had been tethered to this place for years, was gone. Replaced by this lighter, freer Gabriel. His dark eyes, once full of mourning and regret, were lit with a joyous appreciation. As though he dared not hope for this moment.

But it had come, hadn't it? Doubt edged through her.

"Lenore?" she asked, tentative, her throat thick.

"Gone," he said, unwavering.

"And you?" She searched his face, terrified of the answer yet hopeful. "Are you...?"

"Free." The word came out reverent, almost disbelieving.

Her heart clenched. All the emotions she held in check these last few days suddenly exploded out of her. Her throat constricted. Hot tears blurred her vision, spilling before she could stop them.

He caught them on the pad of his thumb, brushing them away with a reverent, unhurried touch.

"You freed me, Victoria."

He gathered her against him again. Her face pressed against his chest, the rough linen of his shirt brushing her cheek. She inhaled the scent of him. That earthy, smokey, leather scent. A scent that was wholly Ravenfell and him. A scent she had not realized until that moment it was both.

"It's over." Her words were muffled against him.

"Yes," he murmured against her hair, his arms holding her tighter, as if he'd never let her go again. "It's over."

Her fingers fisted in the fabric of his shirt, clinging to him. Holding onto this moment that was quiet and reverent and earned. The ache in her palm throbbed, wet and sticky against the linen, and only when she pulled back did she see the smear of red staining the material. Mortification cut through the haze of relief.

"Oh. Your shirt—" Her choked, sounding small and broken, the apology tangled.

But Gabriel's gaze never wavered. "I don't care about the bloody shirt." The words were fierce, final, as if nothing in the world could matter less.

Before she could argue, before she could form another word, his mouth covered hers. His kiss devoured the protest, stealing the breath from her lungs and every thought from her head. It wasn't desperation—it was deliverance. A kiss that branded her, that poured every moment of his longing, his loneliness, his despair into her until she tasted the years of it on his lips. Heat rushed through her veins, dizzying. The world stilled for them alone.

It was a kiss of forever. A kiss of longing. A kiss of reckless abandon.

When he finally broke away, she was gasping, her heart racing, her lips trembling from the force of it. He didn't give her time to falter. Strong hands pulled her upright, steadying her on her weak legs. She blinked into the silence, realizing only then how changed the room was.

A shaft of light from the hallway spilled inside, the only light. The shadows that once danced around them were no longer there. The candles were spent and burned out. The knife was discarded on the floor, forgotten. The strange symbols that glowed and pulsed with life were gone. The chamber, once alive with malice and darkness, was only a room.

Gabriel's touch returned, gentle now, his fingers curling around her wounded hand. He turned it over, thumb brushing over the sticky blood.

"We should bandage this," he murmured, his voice thick, protective. He made to turn toward the door.

"Gabriel, wait." Her words were hesitant as she glanced around the empty room expecting a small figure to appear, expecting to see wet footprints on the floor. There was neither. "What about...Lily?"

His expression shifted, grief creasing his features. "I saw her. After you collapsed." His voice was rough. He swallowed hard, his throat working. "She said you saved her, too. And then she stepped into the light."

Tears blurred her vision again. She blinked them away as the serenity washed through her, stilling the frantic fear that wanted to climb through her. Lily was gone. Free. Safe.

"I'm glad," she whispered, her lips lifting into a smile.

Gabriel slipped an arm around her waist, anchoring her against him. He pressed a kiss against her temple. "Me, too."

Together, they stepped into the hall, leaving the altar room—and everything it had held—behind forever.

As the days passed, Ravenfell itself seemed to exhale. The west wing was boarded up at Gabriel's insistence—to deal with another day, he'd said. Though she suspected it was less about practical repair and more about ensuring neither of them was tempted back into the place where darkness once reigned. She didn't press him. Some wounds needed time before they could be revisited.

But the change was undeniable. The manor was no longer heavy with despair. Sunlight spilled brighter through the tall windows, and the air felt lighter, as though the house itself rejoiced to be free of Lenore's shadow. The silence of the halls was no longer eerie, but serene. For the first time since she arrived, it felt like a home.

And Gabriel...Gabriel had changed too. The brooding shadows that clung to him had softened. He still carried sorrow, yes, but there was something new threaded through him—hope.

One morning, when the sky was a clear and endless blue, they walked together through the gardens. The blooms her mother had once planted swayed in the breeze, vibrant and alive, their perfume curling around her like a benediction. The gravel path crunched beneath their steps. Gabriel's hand was warm in hers, his fingers laced with an assurance that sent a thrum of quiet joy through her chest.

A sharp caw broke the stillness. She glanced up. A raven perched on a branch, its dark eyes glinting as it watched them. Her breath hitched. A shiver, not of fear but of recognition, threaded through her spine. The bird tilted its head, as though judging her, acknowledging her. A Ravenwood, reclaimed.

"It had to be you, you know," Gabriel said, his voice low but certain, as if confessing a thought long held.

She tore her gaze from the raven and turned to him. "What did?"

"The one to break the curse. The one to claim Ravenfell as it was meant to be. Not even your father could do it." His eyes, dark and steady, held her fast.

"Because I'm a descendant?" She trembled with the question, though deep down she knew the answer wasn't that simple.

Gabriel lifted his hands, cupping her face with such tenderness it nearly undid her. His thumbs brushed along her cheeks, grounding her. "Because you are the light." His forehead bent to hers, and his lips whispered over hers, reverent, lingering. Then, barely a breath apart, he murmured, "I love you. Marry me?"

Her heart surged. No hesitation, no doubt. "Yes." The word was a vow, strong and unshakable.

Above them, the raven cawed once more, a final echo in the quiet morning before it spread its wings and soared away. She watched it go, nothing more than a black dot in a brilliant blue sky.

"I love you, too, Gabriel." Her voice broke with the truth of it. Her gaze locked on his, fierce and certain, as the weight of everything they'd endured knit them closer than blood, closer than time.

He pressed a kiss against her forehead and whispered, "Forevermore."

Epilogue

Hilde finished the story of Victoria and Gabriel, leaning heavily into the cushions of the chair. Twilight was upon them and the wind had turned a bit colder as it breezed through the enclosed courtyard. In the distance, the glass chimes sang their melody with the wind.

Fatigue pressed through her with a weariness she hadn't felt in a long while. And it was an effort to maintain her composure so Marigold would not notice. Telling her the story took a lot out of her. And soon she would have to return to her rightful place to fully gather her strength. That meant months away from this mortal realm. Away from Marigold. Something she could no longer avoid. Being here at Willowmere helped, but being in the other realm would fully rejuvenate her.

Opposite her, Marigold sat in the chair with her legs curled under her listening with rapt attention. But her expression was faraway.

"What did you think about that story?" Hilde asked.

"It's sad, isn't it? About Lenore," she said.

She nodded. "Lenore was consumed by her terrible grief. It was hard for her to accept the death of Lily."

Marigold emitted a sigh of contentment. "I'm glad they all found a bit of peace."

"All?" she asked.

"Lenore and Lily. Gabriel and Victoria." Another wistful sigh. "But do curses ever truly end, auntie?"

"Of course, they do, dearest. Love and light pushes back the darkest of shadows." She smiled to reassure her. Darkness and gloom and cursed things never lingered long when true love was in abundance.

A dog barked in the distance along with the hum of traffic on the country road. Night was falling and soon, it would be too dangerous for Marigold to make her way home alone.

"Your mother will be wondering where you are, don't you think?"

Marigold heaved a dramatic sigh. "Mother didn't even tell me you were here. I don't want to go home, yet. Tell me another story."

She chuckled, but knew another story was not in her. She didn't have the strength. "I wish I could but I have to return to my room soon. And you have school tomorrow."

Frowning, Marigold dropped her legs and rose, stretching her arms over her head to ease the tension in her back from sitting so long.

"Next time we see other," Hilde said, "I will tell you another story. If you're not too old for it by then."

"Oh, auntie, I'll never be too old for your stories." She leaned down and kissed her cheek. "Promise me you'll never stop telling them."

"You have my solemn word." She reached for her, squeezing her hand.

Marigold started to go, then turned back, question on her face. "Before I go, can I ask you a question?"

"Of course."

"These stories...where do you get them?"

For a moment, Hilde was stunned to silence. It was something she never expected Marigold to ask, though at fifteen, the girl was far more intelligent and observant than most her age.

She wasn't sure how to answer. Not yet. Because Marigold wouldn't understand since her mother, Linnea, hadn't told her anything of her heritage. Hilde didn't want to be the one to tell her, either—it wasn't her place. It was getting more and more difficult, though, to keep the truth from her.

So, she came up with an answer that held a bit of truth.

"These stories...well, they're not invented, my dear. They're *lived*. And sometimes... sometimes, they ask me to tell them again."

Marigold stared down at her for a long moment, her gaze flickering with hope. And then she giggled. "Aunt Hilde, you make it sound as though these stories are real."

She laughed, too, if only to conceal the truth. Someday, she'd tell Marigold there was another world very near to this one where stories were born, heroes were valiant, and heroines were always brave.

"You best get going, now, love. You don't want to worry your mother."

"Yes, I know I should go. One more thing, though." She twisted her hands together. "Do you think...I mean, will I have a story of my own someday?"

Hilde was unable to stop the grin that erupted. "Oh, I'm sure you will, dearie."

Her face lit with hope and a starry-eyed wonder Hilde felt when she was young. How she envied Marigold. Her niece would one day cross through the veil and become who she was meant to be. She couldn't wait for that day.

Marigold bid her farewell, leaving Hilde there in the gloaming with the faint tinkling of wind chimes. Overhead, the caw of a raven as it flapped through the sky, circled and then flew off. Its black wings disappeared into the evening twilight.

Stories never truly end. They simply wait for the next voice to tell them.

AFTERWORD

Dear Reader,

Welcome to the *Enchanted Realms*, where magic shimmers between the lines and fairy tales are retold with fresh twists, heartfelt romance, and a touch of the unexpected.

You'll notice that each full-length book in this series begins and ends with a special pair of characters—Aunt Hilde and her curious niece, Marigold. These brief scenes serve as a *framing device*, inviting you into the tale and gently guiding you back out again, as if you've just spent an evening curled up beside a fire listening to a beloved story passed down through generations.

Hilde and Marigold are more than just storytellers. Their journey unfolds across the series, each book revealing a little more about who they are, where they come from, and the magic that ties them to the Realms. If you read in order, you'll catch glimpses of their evolving relationship, hidden lore, and maybe even a few secrets that connect everything together.

So settle in, open your heart, and let yourself be swept away. The Realms are waiting.

With love and a pinch of stardust,
Michelle

Acknowledgements

Writing is often a solitary pursuit. We sit at the keyboard chasing words that don't always want to cooperate, hoping to shape them into something worth sharing. It's a joy, a struggle, and everything in between. But along the way, there are always people who make the journey brighter, and I am deeply grateful to them.

First, to **AK Nevermore**, who graciously offered to beta read this book (and traded me one of hers in return!). If you haven't picked up an AK Nevermore novel yet, you should. This woman can write. Beyond her talent, she's also a wonderful, generous human being, and I'm lucky to know her.

To my long-time friend and copyeditor, **Jennifer August**. Thank you for your sharp eye and for giving this story a final polish. But more than that, thank you for your friendship, our margarita lunches, our book talk, our life talk. Love you, girl.

To my big sis, **Kathy**, who patiently beta reads and listens to, well, everything. Your endless support means more than I can say.

And finally, to **you, enchanted readers**. You're the reason I keep telling these stories. Your enthusiasm makes every word worthwhile.

Stories only truly come alive when they're read, shared, and carried in the hearts of readers. Thank you for letting me share a piece of mine with you. May Once Upon a Midnight Dreary haunt you in all the best ways.

Forevermore.

NEXT IN THE SERIES: ONCE UPON A WINTER'S SPELL

A Snow Queen Retelling

Once Upon a Time... in the coldest depths of the far north

A princess cursed by ice. A prince bound by duty. A queen who will stop at nothing to claim them both.

Exiled to the farthest reaches of the north, Princess Anya has spent most of her life hiding her dangerous gift—magic born of winter itself. Feared by her people and hunted by those who crave her power, she lives in solitude behind a wall of ice and sorrow. But when a foreign prince crashes into her life on a diplomatic mission gone wrong, her quiet world begins to thaw.

Prince Soren came seeking a treaty. What he found was a girl of frost and fire and a secret that could ignite a war. Forced into a fragile truce, Anya and Soren must work together to survive assassins, political betrayal, and the Snow Queen herself—Gerda, a ruthless sorceress who wants Anya's crown, her power, and her prince for her own.

As Gerda's icy grip tightens on the realm and Anya's magic spirals out of control, Anya faces an impossible choice—surrender to the cold and become the Snow Queen everyone fears...or risk everything to melt her frozen heart for a prince who was never meant to be hers.

Once Upon a Winter's Spell* is a sweeping fantasy romance filled with elemental magic, slow-burn enemies-to-lovers tension, and the perilous allure of power.

Your Free Book is Waiting!

Step into the Enchanted Realms—Magic and Adventure Await!

A fierce huntress sworn to protect her village. A cursed dire wolf bound by a dark past. And an ancient curse that ties their fates together.

In the heart of the Enchanted Woodlands, where shadows prowl and magic reigns, Poppy is no ordinary girl. Trained by her warrior grandmother, she is the protector of her village, armed with a bow, a sharp mind, and a cloak as red as blood—an heirloom granting her untold power. But when a new terror rises, a fearsome dire wolf known as the Wolf King, Poppy must confront a danger greater than she ever imagined.

Tasked with hunting the beast threatening her home, Poppy soon discovers a dark secret—the Wolf King was once a guardian like her, bound by an ancient curse tied to her own bloodline. Now, Poppy faces an impossible choice—kill the beast and save her people, or break the curse and risk the wrath of the village she has sworn to protect.

With the fate of both worlds hanging in the balance, Poppy must decide what kind of huntress she truly is.

Part of the Enchanted Realms world. Perfect for fans of fierce heroines, cursed beasts, and slow-burn fantasy romance set in lush, magical forests.

Get a free copy of Once Upon an Ancient Curse, An Enchanted Realms Novella. *Available to newsletter subscribers only*

https://viplist.michellemiles.net/enchanted

ALSO BY MICHELLE MILES

Age of Wizards (Epic Fantasy)

In the Tower of the Wizard King

On the Hunt for the Wizard King

Dragon Protectors (Paranormal Shifter Romance)

Desiring the Dragon Lord

Seducing the Dragon Knight

Tempting Her Dragon Bodyguard

Dragon Protectors Book Collection, Books 1-3

Dream Walker (Urban Fantasy)

Call of the Dark

Blood and Bone

Flame and Fury

Smoke and Ashes

Light of the World

Dream Walker Collection (Books 1-5)

Divin Heir: Dream Walker Origins

Enchanted Realms (YA Fantasy Romance)

Once Upon a Midnight Clear (Cinderella)

Once Upon True Love's Kiss (Snow White)

Once Upon an Enchanted Kiss (Sleeping Beauty)

Once Upon an Enchanted Castle (Beauty & the Beast)

Once Upon a Midnight Dreary (Poe's The Raven)

Enchanted Realms Related Novellas

Once Upon an Ancient Curse (Red Riding Hood)

Once Upon a Silver Strand (Rapunzel)

Once Upon a Woven Wish (Rumpelstiltskin)

Five Towers (YA Fantasy)

The Sorcerer's Daughter

Highland Destiny (Paranormal Romance)

Desiring the Highland Laird

Loving the Highland Warrior

Captivating the Highland Rogue

Legends of the Five Crowns (Romantasy)

with Misty Evans

The Lost Kingdom

The Flame and the Dragon

**Ransom & Fortune Adventures
(Time Travel Action/Adventure)**

Highland Fling, Vol 1

Dead of Winter, Vol 2

The Citadel, Vol 3

Lord of the Underworld, Vol 4

Realm of Honor (Fantasy Romance)

One Knight Only

Only for a Knight

A Knight to Remember

A Knight Like No Other

Shadows of the Knight

Realm of Honor Collection (Books 1-5)

Shorts and Anthologies (Fantasy/Paranormal)
Newsletter Subscribers Only

A Dance Among the Faeries, A Short Story

Eorwulf, A Short Story

Dragons of Emhain, Short Story Collection

Watch for more at www.MichelleMiles.net
Buy Direct at www.MichelleMilesBooks.com

About the Author

MICHELLE MILES believes every story should have a little magic, a dash of danger, and a whole lot of heart. She writes fantasy, paranormal, and young adult adventures filled with fierce heroines, unforgettable heroes, and the kind of romance that makes you believe in happily-ever-after. From angels and demons to dragons, elves, and time travelers, her books invite readers into worlds brimming with epic quests, high stakes, and enchanting possibilities.

When she's not crafting new adventures, Michelle lends her voice to other authors' worlds as a narrator and hosts Miles Beyond the Page, a podcast where writers share the triumphs and challenges of their creative journeys. A proud Texan, she loves getting lost in a good book, exploring hiking trails, watching her favorite movies, and savoring a glass of wine while dreaming up her next tale.

**Magical Worlds, Daring Adventures,
Unforgettable Romance!**

Read more at www.MichelleMiles.net
Buy Direct at www.MichelleMilesBooks.com

www.ingramcontent.com/pod-product-compliance
Lightning Source LLC
Chambersburg PA
CBHW071238300726
48975CB00002B/469